O9-BUD-684

A large hand wrapped around her wrist and prevented her from impersonating a flipped pancake.

Awareness prickled up her arm from the strong hand around her wrist. Her gaze lifted all the way up to a pair of dark sexy eyes. Her heart stumbled worse than her feet and air sprinted from her lungs like a that of a runner's. Isaiah Reynolds.

The lean muscles of his arms were bared by a sleeveless red athletic shirt. Basketball shorts partially covered sculpted legs long enough to make a redwood jealous. If a tree could get jealous. The spice of sweat and his own masculine scent swirled through her senses and made her knees wobbly. Recognition brightened his warm brown eyes. For a split second he seemed happy and surprised right before his brows furled. His lips, the lower one fuller and so damn kissable, twisted into a frown.

"Angel?" he said in a tenor tone that was as smooth as silk and ran over her just as seductively.

SHERWOOD FOREST LIBRARY
7117 W. SEVEN MILE RD.
DETROIT, MI 48221

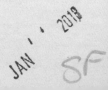
JAN   2019
SF

Dear Reader,

Thank you for spending your time with my characters today. When I first introduced Isaiah in *Full Court Seduction*, I knew I had to write a story for him. The so-called "good guy" of the team needed a woman to make him put all his rules aside in the name of love. Angela "Angel" did exactly that. She's not what he planned for, nor did he expect their first introduction to cause so much change in his life. Angela has been hit with some hard blows, but she remains upbeat and optimistic. Her refusal to let circumstances beat her down is one of the reasons Isaiah can't help but fall for her.

I hope you enjoy their road to happily-ever-after. Please be sure to leave a review or drop me an email at synithia@synithiawilliams.com and let me know what you think.

Happy reading!

Synithia W.

OVERTIME FOR LOVE

SYNITHIA WILLIAMS

HARLEQUIN® KIMANI™ ROMANCE

If you purchased this book without a cover you should be aware that this book is stolen property. It was reported as "unsold and destroyed" to the publisher, and neither the author nor the publisher has received any payment for this "stripped book."

Recycling programs
for this product may
not exist in your area.

ISBN-13: 978-1-335-21652-6

Overtime for Love

Copyright © 2018 by Synithia R. Williams

All rights reserved. The reproduction, transmission or utilization of this work in whole or in part in any form by any electronic, mechanical or other means, now known or hereinafter invented, including xerography, photocopying and recording, or in any information storage or retrieval system, is forbidden without written permission. For permission please contact Harlequin Kimani, 225 Duncan Mill Road, Toronto, Ontario M3B 3K9, Canada.

This is a work of fiction. Names, characters, places and incidents are either the product of the author's imagination or are used fictitiously, and any resemblance to actual persons, living or dead, business establishments, events or locales is entirely coincidental.

® and TM are trademarks of Harlequin Enterprises Limited or its corporate affiliates. Trademarks indicated with ® are registered in the United States Patent and Trademark Office, the Canadian Intellectual Property Office and in other countries.

For questions and comments about the quality of this book please contact us at CustomerService@Harlequin.com.

HARLEQUIN®

Printed in U.S.A.

www.Harlequin.com

Synithia Williams has been an avid romance-novel lover since picking up her first at the age of thirteen. It was only natural that she would begin penning her own romances soon after—much to the chagrin of her high school math teachers. She's a native of South Carolina and now writes romances as hot as their southern settings. Outside of writing, she works on water quality and sustainability issues for local government. She's married to her own personal hero, and they have two sons who've convinced her that professional wrestling and superheroes are supreme entertainment. When she isn't working, writing, or being a wife and mother, she's usually bingeing on TV series, playing around on social media or planning her next girls' night out with friends. You can learn more about Synithia by visiting her website, www.synithiawilliams.com, where she blogs about writing, life and relationships.

Books by Synithia Williams

Harlequin Kimani Romance

A New York Kind of Love
A Malibu Kind of Romance
Full Court Seduction
Overtime for Love

Acknowledgments

Thank you to the great team at Harlequin Kimani: Shannon Criss and Keyla Hernandez. You two helped tighten my stories, always answered my questions and were super helpful during my time with Kimani. I wish you much success in your future endeavors.

Chapter 1

Bless the soul of the person who invented air-conditioning.

Angela Bouler sighed in ecstasy when she opened the door to the North Region Activity Center and cool air kissed her skin. Heat and humidity had combined to make summer in Jacksonville, Florida, beat Hell on the hot and uncomfortable scale. She leaned back against the open door and turned to her only nephew, who was coming up behind her. Oblivious to the heat, and enthralled by his cell phone, Cory walked slower than a two-legged tortoise.

"Come on, Cory. Whatever is on that thing will still be there once we're inside the air-conditioned building." Her attempt at an upbeat tone wilted.

After scrambling to get off work early so she could pick up Cory from her neighbor and get him to the activity center in time to sign up for a month-long basketball camp, in the middle of a heat wave straight from the pits of Hell, she didn't feel too bad about not being perky. She'd left the blazer she'd worn to her day job as a court-appointed advocate for foster children in the car, but even without the extra layer, her blouse stuck to her back and tendrils of hair escaped the ponytail she'd swept her thick shoulder-length hair into and clung to her neck.

Cory slipped his phone into the pocket of his basketball shorts and picked up his speed to match that of a three-legged tortoise. "I'm hungry," he grumbled.

"You're always hungry."

"I'm growing. I'm almost a man now," he said with a cocky, know-it-all smile perfected by teenagers everywhere.

Angela rolled her eyes but didn't suppress her grin. "Whatever, *man*. Pay me back for the box of Hot Pockets you ate in one day."

"I said almost a man. I'm broke." Cory grinned and looked so much like her brother Angela's heart hurt. He was as tall as she was, but would probably grow several more inches. Despite his slow pace, his skin, the color of dark honey, held a red flush from the heat.

Angela ruffled his purposefully messy high-top fade, then gently pushed him farther into the cool building. Cory tried not to laugh and brushed her hand away. Ever since her brother's girlfriend, Heather, had dropped off Cory at Angela's door a month ago, saying nothing more than "I can't take him to New York—he'll ruin my chance at a stage career," Cory had done nothing but eat, eat and then eat more, all while growing half an inch every fifteen minutes. Her fifteen-hundred-square-foot apartment felt like five hundred and if she didn't hide her good ice cream in an old bag of frozen peas she'd have nothing to eat. Though she suspected Cory's never-ending appetite would eventually lead him to explore the frozen veggies and discover her hiding place.

She closed the door and directed Cory toward the main desk. "Come on. Let's get you signed up. This will be fun!" She managed legit excitement with the last statement.

The grin on Cory's face melted away. Another thing

she was learning about thirteen-year-old boys—they went from happy to sullen in a split second. "This is charity."

"A favor isn't charity. One of the boys originally registered for camp dropped out and my boss was nice enough to let me sign you up. There are plenty of other kids we work with who would love to be in your place. Do you want me to tell my boss to give the registration to another kid?"

Her office got five registrations to the activity center's coveted camp with the Jacksonville Gators professional basketball team. Angela hadn't asked for Cory to get the newly opened spot, but couldn't turn it down when her boss approached her at the last minute. Cory deserved some joy. Her brother, Darryl, was serving time for embezzling funds at his job—the idiot—and his mom had up and left for New York. Angela refused to be another person who let him down. She would do whatever she could to make Cory feel wanted. Even though she had no idea what she was doing. Kids hadn't been in her short- or long-term plans.

Cory stuffed his hands into his pockets and shook his head. "No."

"Then zip it and let's get you registered." Angela rubbed his back and smiled.

She understood his aversion to accepting things. Help from others usually came with a price. Something she'd learned after her parents died and her aunt considered the money Angela's parents left for Angela and her brother's college educations to be her "reward" for taking in the kids. After that lesson, Angela chose to rely on herself to get what she wanted out of life. She'd taken a job as a bartender at a gentlemen's club to pay for her undergraduate degree and continued serving drinks part-time after landing the position as an advocate to help cover the costs of graduate school. She paid her own way and was proud of that, but a coveted spot in a basketball camp with professionals was an exception to her don't-accept-help rule.

She looked around the inside of the activity center. The large one-story building was filled with light from the multitude of windows along the front. It housed a gymnasium, rooms for various exercise and art classes, and a large meeting space. A table next to one of the classrooms had a sign that identified it as the spot to register for the Gators' basketball camp.

They signed in at the desk and were directed inside, where twenty other kids and their parents and guardians sat waiting. She and Cory found a seat toward the front. Angela spotted and waved at the program director, Keri Little. Keri was a petite firecracker of a woman with mocha skin and natural red hair cut into a short tapered style. Angela often spoke with Keri when recommending kids from their office to the program.

Keri moved to the front of the room and tapped on the desk to get everyone's attention. The hum of conversation disappeared and Keri gave the room a hundred-watt smile.

"Good afternoon! First, I want to thank you all for taking time out of your busy schedules to come to the orientation for the Jacksonville Gators' basketball camp. This is going to be a great year, not only because I know we've got a great group of kids, but also because our Gators are league champions!"

Keri cheered and many of the parents and kids joined in. Cory sat up straighter. Excitement crept into his light brown eyes. Angela felt a rush of satisfaction. Finally, a show of interest.

"I know an orientation for a basketball camp may seem odd," Keri continued, "but believe me, after partnering with the Gators for seven years to bring this program together, there are a lot of things we want to make sure we let parents and kids know. Plus, this year we have a few changes. Each year, Coach Gray lets me know which players will be participating in the camp. If you look in your packet, you'll see a list of the players attending and when they'll be here. Coach Gray just informed me that this year's host player will be none other than star forward Isaiah Reynolds!"

Another murmur went through the crowd as a quick flash of excitement surged through Angela. She couldn't serve drinks in a popular gentlemen's club and not have come across a few members of the Gators team. As the team's "good guy," Isaiah was typically an exception to the rule, but he'd come in after the team won the championship and they all came in to celebrate at the club.

To her surprise, he'd hung out at the bar instead of making it rain hundred-dollar bills in the VIP section. She'd served him drinks. He'd asked about her tribal tattoo, an African symbol of strength, on her wrist. Not in the creepy, I'm-trying-to-fake-interest-to-hook-up-with-you way she often got. He'd seemed genuinely interested. Before long, they'd struck up a conversation that never lapsed or grew stale, even when she walked away to serve other customers. She'd felt a connection, so much so that she'd debated whether to give him her number if he wanted it, but he'd left without asking.

She'd been a little disappointed, but things happened for a reason. Isaiah not asking for her number had probably been for the best. Most guys who hit on her at the club only wanted a quick hookup. Not her style. That didn't stop the flutter of her heart at the thought of seeing him again.

"I know we're all very excited to be interacting with

such talented players, but please remember, they're here for the camp—not for socializing. We're very protective of their privacy," Keri said, as if she could sense the anticipation jolting through Angela.

Angela's face heated even though Keri wasn't looking at her. She was here for Cory. One cool conversation with Isaiah wasn't important.

Keri's smile shifted to a look of determination. "One of the reasons this program works so well is because of the rules. So here they are. There will be plenty of opportunities for you and your kids to take pictures with the players. So please, no selfies, unsolicited shots, or requests for pictures. Do not ask for autographs. The players will give each kid an autographed jersey at the end of camp. No asking for money." Keri held up a hand when a few parents, including Angela, chuckled in surprise. "I know that sounds obvious, but we've had people try. And again, please respect boundaries—parents, that also means no *fraternizing* with the players, if you know what I mean. Violation of any of these rules will result in your child's immediate withdrawal from the program."

The lady next to Angela tapped her with her elbow. "Too bad, huh?"

Angela gave her a weak smile. When she looked at Cory he snickered with a hand over his mouth. "Why are you laughing?"

"*Fraternizing* with a player?" He wiggled his eyebrows.

Angela rolled her eyes and shook her head. "You don't have to worry about that."

Keri went through more of the rules. Angela pulled the papers out of the packet and skimmed through them. Despite the brief moment of excitement when she'd learned Isaiah would be at the camp, she really didn't want to interact with the players. That would limit the possibility of them connecting *Angel* the bartender to Angela Bouler the advocate. She wasn't ashamed of her bartending job, but her supervisor in the advocacy office thought the fact that she also worked at a strip club was best kept under the radar. Their director was ultraconservative, and he wouldn't want any hint of a scandal.

A player recognizing her didn't necessarily mean word of her part-time job would get back to their director, but to be sure, she'd limit her interactions. Drop off Cory in the morning, pick him up after work, and that was it. She could admire Isaiah Reynolds from afar and come up with silly fantasies of what might've happened if he'd asked for her number. She wouldn't risk her job or Cory's shot at some happiness just to talk to Isaiah Reynolds again.

Chapter 2

Isaiah watched the tattoo needle scrape across the upper arm of his teammate and friend Kevin Kouky and grimaced. "I can't believe I let you talk me into coming here."

Kevin grinned at Isaiah from a seat in his favorite tattoo parlor. "You know you want one."

Isaiah only grunted and shifted in his own seat. Kevin and the tattoo artist, Jack, both chuckled. Isaiah ignored them and studied the pictures of the elaborate tattoos on the wall. Skin Ink was one of the biggest and best tattoo parlors in the Jacksonville area. Most of the members of the Jacksonville Gators basketball team got their art there.

Isaiah had no idea how many tattoos Kevin had in total. His arms, chest and part of his neck were covered with colorful designs. Today he filled in a blank spot on his right forearm with a picture of the championship trophy and the date. He'd told Isaiah the spot was saved for that reason. Kevin was thirty-five and one of the oldest members of the team, even though his colorful tattoos and even more colorful attitude made people think he was younger. He'd waited a long time to win a championship and even though Isaiah never wanted a tattoo himself, he was happy to watch Kevin fill in the spot. Well…willing to watch.

"I don't see the point of scarring my body unnecessarily." Isaiah repeated the words his dad often said whenever he saw tattoos on a person. He tugged uncomfortably on his white polo shirt. His mother and father were both college professors, in engineering and chemistry, respectively. They weren't big fans of art, which definitely included body art. Isaiah had once felt the same, but after years playing basketball in college and professionally, he'd come to appreciate good body art—at least, on someone else.

Kevin looked down at the needle marking his arm. "Each tat has a reason. When you have a good reason, you'll get one."

Isaiah had flirted with the idea of getting a tattoo before, but hadn't thought of anything he liked enough to permanently emblazon on his pecan-brown skin. Maybe the chemical symbol for testosterone or a differential equation. His parents might not freak out over a chemical bond or engineering nod versus a picture of the championship trophy. The idea made him smile even though he'd never do it. He no longer did things that would shock or disappoint his parents.

His cell phone chimed. Isaiah checked his email, then looked at Kevin. "Ms. Keri from the activity center sent over the agenda. You still helping with the camp this year?"

"Of course," Kevin said in an eager voice. "Best time of the year. Thanks for inviting me again."

Isaiah turned his chair around and straddled it with his arms resting on the back. "From what I heard, the kids loved you last year. Why wouldn't I?"

"I know you think I'm wild," Kevin said with a grin.

Isaiah laughed. "That's why I hang out with you."

Isaiah would rather have Kevin there than any of his other teammates. He and Kevin were total opposites. Kevin was the wild card on the team with tattoos, earrings and a spontaneous personality that had led to two failed long-term relationships and four kids. Isaiah had the reserved nature cultivated by academic parents, spent more time volunteering than partying and had limited experience with women, including one on-again, off-again relationship with his college girlfriend, Bridget, and a few hookups in between. Despite their differences, their personalities jibed. Mostly because Isaiah lived vicariously through Kevin. His friend wasn't afraid to say, do, or go for what he wanted, whereas Isaiah spent more time thinking of long-term consequences instead of immediate needs. Nearly ruining his mother's career due to a rash decision had that kind of long-term effect.

Isaiah checked the schedule for the basketball camp and compared it to his schedule, saw a conflict and grunted. "I'm going to miss picking up Bridget from the airport," he said absently.

"And? She can't find her way to a hotel?" Kevin asked drily.

Kevin had met Bridget twice and wasn't a fan. Isaiah wasn't offended. Bridget's straightforward personality often rubbed people the wrong way. For the past year, she and Isaiah had been off-again while she finished law school. He'd asked her to move to Jacksonville after getting her degree. He was tired of being on the dating scene. He was ready for a wife and kids. Bridget was the best option. His parents liked her, they were compatible and he knew she wasn't after him because he was a professional baller.

Isaiah flipped his phone in his hand. "I thought about letting her stay at my place," he said in a blasé tone.

Kevin's attention snapped to Isaiah. "Hell no!"

Isaiah shrugged. "Why not?"

"Her staying with you means you're back on again."

"I'm ready for that step."

Kevin cocked his head to the side. "What step?"

"The next step. Marriage, kids, all that."

Kevin's head shook before Isaiah finished talking. "Not her."

He hadn't expected Kevin to give an enthusiastic endorsement for Bridget, but he wasn't expecting the flat-out steel in his friend's voice. "Why not?"

"Man, she's a nice girl but she isn't right for you."

Isaiah leaned back and laughed. "She's perfect for me. Smart. Beautiful. Good family. No scandals."

Kevin's head fell back and he made a snoring sound. "Boring."

Isaiah grinned at his friend's theatrics. "Reliable. I'd much rather trust my future with her than someone I don't know. You know how exhausting dating is? I don't want to meet some new woman's mom, dad, sisters and brothers. I don't want to have to figure out if she's really into me or hoping to be the next star of celebrity wives. I know and trust Bridget."

"You can trust her to tie your balls in a knot," Kevin grumbled. "And not in the good way."

Isaiah raised a brow. "There's a good way?"

Jack stopped the tattoo gun to stare at Isaiah. "Of course there's a good way."

Isaiah waved a hand. "Oh, well, then enlighten me."

Kevin pointed at Isaiah with his free hand. "You want a woman who drives you crazy and makes you laugh. Someone who heats your blood with just a look.

A woman that'll cuss you out when you're being a fool, but you know she'll always have your back."

"That sounds like a recipe for drama." Isaiah couldn't keep the distaste out of his voice.

"It's a recipe for excitement," Kevin said. "She challenges you, pushes you, and you might not like it all the time, you may argue, but making up again?" Kevin grinned and nodded. "That makes everything worth it."

Isaiah laughed. "No harm, but that doesn't sound like the type of marriage I want."

"Hell, what can I say? That didn't work for my marriage, either." Kevin said in a teasing voice, but Isaiah caught the glimpse of regret in his eye.

Kevin had married his college sweetheart and she'd divorced him after five years. Then he'd had another long-term relationship that had ended a few years ago. He'd admitted to his mistakes in those relationships, and joked about being a failure at long-term commitment. The only good thing he claimed from his rocky relationships was his kids. Even though he often joked about his past, Isaiah suspected his failed relationships hurt more than he let on.

"But we're not talking about me," Kevin said, his cheerful voice back. "You're champing at the bit to find a wife and have a pack of kids. I get it—your parents have a beautiful union and you like stability. You're *that* guy."

"*That* guy?" Isaiah asked.

"The relationship guy. That's cool. We need guys like you out there. It's good for team testosterone to have decent men out there, but don't let your visions of a perfect family lead you to marrying the wrong woman. Divorce isn't fun. Believe me."

"Bridget isn't the wrong woman. That's why I asked her to move to Jacksonville. When I get married I want to stay married. I know Bridget and she knows me. We both want the same things and our families love each other. She's perfect."

Jack glanced at Isaiah quickly before going back to the tattoo. "Perfect doesn't mean you want to *sleep* with her every night."

Heat filled Isaiah's face and he flipped his cell phone again. "We're compatible in every way if that's what you're getting at."

It had been a while since they'd slept together. And the last time had been rushed, when they'd both been in the same city a year ago and only had a few hours before she had to catch a flight. He'd always thought their sex life was decent, until he'd heard the stories the guys told. Then he realized his and Bridget's sex life had always been tame. There was nothing wrong with tame... it just made him wonder about wild.

Kevin shook his head. "Big deal. Most women are decent in bed. She's moving here because you asked her to. Are you burning to see her in here?" Kevin placed a fist over his heart. "Is she all up in your head? Are you twisting, turning and downright yearning for her to get here so you can get your arms around her?"

Twisting and turning, yes. But not out of anticipation. More out of a sense of anxiety. Was asking her here the right thing? That wasn't something to talk about now. Kevin was his friend, but Jack didn't need insight on Isaiah's boring romantic life. "Of course," he said quickly. Kevin's look said Isaiah was full of crap.

Isaiah focused on his phone and checked social media. He thought about the last time a woman had heated his blood. *Still thinking about Angel.* Isaiah clenched the phone and his teeth. He needed to stop thinking of Angel, but not thinking of her was nearly impossible. Dark sparkling eyes, full luscious lips, curves... Damn, the woman's curves were amazing. Smooth, golden tan skin that had sparkled with a glittery lotion that smelled as enticing as she looked. And that thick dark hair—he'd wanted to reach out and touch it.

Angel was the perfect name. If that was her real name. The bartender at Sweethearts gentlemen's club probably used a fake name, just like the dancers did.

Their conversation had lasted all night. He'd felt a connection, but wasn't that supposed to be what he felt? Women at the strip club worked to make connections so patrons spent more money. Even though he'd wanted to ask for her number, he'd made himself walk away instead of shattering the illusion if she turned him down.

"What are you guys doing tonight?" Isaiah asked.

"Some of the fellas are going to Sweethearts. I'm not feeling it. I'd rather burn my money on something else."

The jump shot of anticipation at the mention of Sweethearts made Isaiah's heart dribble against his rib cage. He took a slow breath to steady the beat. He didn't need to go back there.

"Why aren't you feeling it?" Isaiah asked.

"I promised Chanel I'd take her to Hawaii."

Kevin's latest fling. Isaiah cocked his head and smirked at Kevin. "She give you the burning feeling you were telling me about?"

"Hell no. Chanel is only looking for a good time. That's all I'm good for." Before Isaiah could comment on the grim tone of his friend's admission, Kevin got a knowing look in his gray eyes. "Are *you* going to the club?"

Isaiah grunted and shook his head. "Nah. What for?"

Kevin just grinned. He'd teased Isaiah about Angel for a week after the team celebrated at Sweethearts.

Teased him and called him a damn fool for not getting her number. According to Will Hampton, another friend and teammate, her not giving him her number was unlikely. Perks of being a professional athlete, he'd said, but Will was the type of guy not many women said no to.

Isaiah wasn't going to bring Angel back into the conversation. Bad enough her sexy laugh and beautiful smile still popped up in his dreams. "You'll be back from Hawaii in time for camp?" He stood and looked at the pictures on the wall.

"Just going for a weekend. I'll be back," Kevin said.

One of the pictures on the wall caught Isaiah's attention. He walked over for a closer look. The five curved lines arranged in a star shape reminded him of the tattoo Angel had on her wrist. The African symbol for strength.

A reminder that I can handle anything that comes my way. I'm strong enough to take care of me.

Her voice had held a trace of some lingering pain. He'd wanted to know what it was so he could wipe it clean away. But he'd changed the subject. Teased that he would get a shark tattoo because it was his favorite animal. She'd laughed and he'd fallen into her spell.

Too bad life wasn't just about going with instinct, the way a shark did. Instinct would have him back at the club tonight. There were consequences to consider. Plans to be made. Plans that didn't involve falling for a bartender with a beautiful smile after already asking the "perfect" woman to move to his town and talk about their future.

Chapter 3

Angela fought to keep the professional smile on her face as she listened to the volunteer sitting across from her desk give another excuse for not visiting the child she was assigned to this month. Olivia Parker was a decent lady. She was retired from the school system, had friendly brown eyes and a matronly appearance. She'd heard about the need for advocates when Angela's supervisor was interviewed by the local news six months ago and immediately came in to volunteer. Except she always had an excuse for why she couldn't put in the time.

Everyone in the office was assigned a group of volunteers to organize and ensure the kids they represented had someone to check in on them. Angela's volunteers rarely missed visits because she was constantly touching base with them. Ms. Parker was her coworker Jerry's volunteer. He'd asked her to deal with Ms. Parker because he "couldn't be mean to someone who reminded him of his grandmother." The real excuse: he didn't know how to manage his volunteers.

"You understand, Angela, why I didn't make it this month. Between my husband getting sick, the drama with my sister and Pickle's surgery, it just slipped my mind," Olivia said in a pleading voice.

Angela took a deep breath. Pickle was Ms. Parker's miniature schnauzer. "I do understand, but it is also very important that our volunteers personally see their assigned child every month. That's the only way we can ensure they're adapting to their new foster home and are making any scheduled court appearances or visits with their parents. I'll work with Jerry to cover your visit tomorrow, but please let Jerry know ahead of time if you can't make next month's visit."

Olivia bobbed her head up and down. "No. No. I'll go first thing in the morning. I understand and I promise I won't miss next month. I'll be sure to visit not just once, but—"

"Twice." Angela forced her smile to remain. "I know." She glanced at the clock and stood. This meeting with Ms. Parker had gone past five o'clock. Angela needed to be out of the office and on the road right at five to dodge the worst of the traffic before picking up Cory and getting him back to her apartment, where her neighbor, Nate, watched him while she worked nights at Sweethearts.

Angela stood, which prompted Ms. Parker to do so, as well. Ms. Parker liked to talk and she would easily go on for another thirty minutes about her dog and husband if Angela didn't end the conversation. "Thanks again for your service, Ms. Parker. We can't look out for the kids without the dedication of volunteers like you."

Ms. Parker blushed and nodded and said again how sorry she was as Angela ushered her out of the office. Why people like Ms. Parker would go through the rigorous training and background checks necessary to volunteer with the child advocacy office only to flake out on responsibilities every other month didn't make much sense to Angela. It was a constant source of frustration. The kids were the ones who suffered; things were missed when there wasn't consistent contact with them. Angela knew because she'd lived it. If she'd had someone looking out for her after her parents died, maybe her aunt wouldn't have found it so easy to steal her inheritance. That was the reason she'd gone into social work. She wanted to make sure no other kid was taken advantage of by the people who were supposed to protect them.

She poked her head into Jerry's office, which was next to hers, but he wasn't there. A quick check with the admin assistant and she learned Jerry was gone for the day.

"He did tell me to thank you for handling Ms. Parker," Martha said.

Angela bit back her annoyance and took a deep breath. At least Ms. Parker had been reprimanded, and hopefully wouldn't neglect her duties next month. Angela went back to her office, powered down her computer and scooped up her purse. Ten after five. Maybe enough time to hit the road and get to Cory before the activity center charged her for being late picking him up. It was his first week of basketball camp. She didn't want to be late the first day and start off as "that parent."

Somebody in heaven liked her because Angela arrived at the activity center at exactly five-twenty-nine. She jumped out of the car and raced into the building. The young guy working the front desk smiled and didn't charge her for being two minutes late by their clock, then directed her to the gym, where Cory was waiting. She thanked the guy, glanced at her watch and hurried to the gym. Okay, pick up Cory, drive like a maniac back home, thank Nate again for being an awesome neighbor and get to second job.

Angela grabbed the door to the gym and pulled. Someone shoved the door from the other side and she stumbled back. Her heels slipped on the floor. A large hand wrapped around her wrist and prevented her from impersonating a flipped pancake.

Awareness prickled up her arm from the strong hand around her wrist. Her gaze lifted all the way up to a pair of dark, sexy eyes. Her heart stumbled worse than her feet and air sprinted from her lungs like an Olympic runner. Isaiah Reynolds.

He was wearing a sleeveless red athletic shirt, so the lean muscles of his arms were bared. Basketball shorts partially covered sculpted legs long enough to make a redwood jealous. If a tree could get jealous. The spice of sweat and his own masculine scent swirled through her senses and made her knees wobbly. Recognition brightened his warm brown eyes. For a split second, he seemed happy and surprised, then his brow furrowed and his lips, the lower one fuller and so damn kissable, twisted into a frown.

"Angel?" he said in a tone that was as smooth as silk and ran over her just as seductively.

Angela swallowed hard and tried to ignore the heat spreading through her body. She wanted him, which meant she had to avoid him at all costs for the remainder of the camp. Otherwise he'd have her with a crook of his finger and a smile.

Isaiah's fingers tightened around Angel's small wrist. He'd recognized her instantly. Gone were the sparkly white angel wings she wore behind the bar at Sweethearts. A tasteful gray button-up shirt replaced the white tank top he'd last seen her in, although the garment still hugged her perfectly rounded breasts. A fitted black pencil skirt silhouetted full hips instead of tight black pants. No glittery makeup enhanced her eyes, which were so brown and deep he could forget the world while holding her gaze. Perfect lips parted and the sweet scent of flowers surrounded him.

He wanted to draw her closer. He'd thought of her constantly after their conversation at the bar that night. The excitement of literally bumping into her again nearly made him step closer, breathe in her soft perfume, get lost in her eyes. Why was she here?

"Angela." Her low seductive voice broke through his daze.

He blinked. "What?"

"My name is Angela. Not Angel."

Of course. Angel suited her better, though. Her lips curved into a hesitant smile that snatched his ability to think. To breathe. Talk.

Man, he hated this. Seeing her made him feel like the awkward, tongue-tied teenager he used to be. The quiet kid who didn't know how to talk to girls. Put a basketball in his hands, get him in front of a crowd of reporters discussing his latest game or business venture, and he knew exactly what to do. Have a pretty woman he liked smile at him and his voice box disconnected from his brain.

She was really here. And now she was frowning. Which meant he was just staring instead of talking.

Isaiah let go of her wrist and took a step back. "What are you doing here?" Props to him for keeping his voice normal. Maturity had at least given him the ability to hide his discomfort better.

"Aunt Angela, you know Isaiah Reynolds?" Cory, the boy Isaiah had quickly noticed during the camp, spoke up. Cory had been quiet, a bit sullen, especially when the girls in the camp were around, but he was great with a basketball. Reminded Isaiah a little of himself. Maybe more than a little.

Isaiah looked at the young boy, then back at Angel… Angela. "This is your aunt?"

Cory nodded. Angela reached for the silver charm on her necklace and played with it. Her slim fingers brushed the smooth caramel skin of her chest exposed by the V-neck opening of her blouse. That night in the bar, the lace edges of a black bra peaked out from the scooped neckline of her tank top. Was she wearing a lace bra today? He was tall enough. All he'd have to do is lean a little toward her and he'd be able to see down that V…

Isaiah took another step back. *What the hell? You're not Cory's age. No staring down her blouse.*

"I am," Angela said.

An uneasy thought crept into Isaiah's brain. People went to great lengths just to be close to a professional athlete. He may still occasionally get tongue-tied around a beautiful woman, but he wasn't stupid.

"Did you—did you sign him up…because of me?"

Her eyes widened for a second. Her hand dropped from the necklace. She slowly turned to Cory. "Can you go wait for me by the car?"

Cory raised an eyebrow. "What for?"

"Because I said so. Now go to the car."

Cory let out a heavy sigh. "Fine. 'Bye, Mr. Reynolds." He waved, then shuffled away, mumbling something under his breath.

Angela glared at her nephew's back. When he was out of earshot, she turned her sharp gaze Isaiah's way. She stepped to the side of the door of the gym and he followed so they wouldn't be so out in the open.

"Did you really just accuse me of bringing Cory here because of you?"

The disbelief in her tone sounded sincere. But he'd

been in the league for seven years and he'd heard all kinds of "sincerity" from exuberant fans before.

"It's a fair question."

"It's an insulting question." Anger sparked in her brown eyes. "And a very egotistical one."

"Egotistical?"

She crossed her arms over her chest. "Why in the world would I stalk you? Much less, use my nephew to do that?"

"I once had a man break his son's arm so I would come visit him in the hospital. I've had people do crazy things to try and get close to me."

That doused the flames in her eyes. "Seriously? Someone would do something like that to his own son?"

He wished it wasn't true. For every hundred normal fans there was always one crazy one that took things too far. "Fans can be crazy."

The tightness of her crossed arms loosened and the tension in her stance relaxed. "Look, the organization I work for has five slots for this camp every year. One of the kids we chose had to back out at the last minute. My boss offered the space to Cory."

He cocked his head to the side. "Sweethearts?" he asked skeptically.

She shook her head and the corners of her lips rose slightly. "That's my part-time job. I work full-time in an office that manages court-appointed advocates for kids."

That explained her business attire today, and Keri had told him they'd had one substitution from the advocacy center. Still. "Will you always be picking up Cory, or will his parents…?"

The tension returned to her face and stance. "Just me. It's a long story," she said in a voice that told him she had no desire to get into it. "I promise this isn't some crazy fangirl thing. I know you hear that a lot, but it's true. I didn't even know you'd be hosting until registration. When I found out, I promised myself I'd stay away from you."

"Why?"

She shifted her stance and slid the strap of her black purse farther up her shoulder. "Because there aren't many people who know where I serve drinks. I don't need that getting back to my boss."

He believed her. Which was crazy. He didn't really know her, but despite the vibe he'd felt when he'd first met her, she hadn't struck him as the type to seek him out. She'd been cool, easy to talk to and only a little flirty, but she'd also seemed like her life would go on after he walked out the door. It was one of the reasons he'd thought of her so much.

"Are you ashamed of where you work?"

Her shoulders straightened. "Absolutely not. Are you saying I should be?"

He held up his hands in defense. "No."

She relaxed and tilted her head, thick strands of her hair sliding over her shoulder. "I'm surprised you thought I signed him up to see you again. I didn't think you'd remember me."

"I couldn't forget you."

Her luscious lips parted and she sucked in a breath. Isaiah's face heated. *Way to go, Isaiah.*

"I mean, you were wearing angel wings."

She lowered her lashes and chuckled. "Yeah, they do get people's attention." She peeked at him from beneath long lashes. He felt trapped by the warm depths of her eyes. Damn, she was fine.

Angela blinked, breaking eye contact. "I've really got

to go." She pointed toward the door. "I promise I won't stalk you or anything. You won't even see me."

"I wouldn't mind seeing you."

Her eyes widened. Her smile brightened just a little before regret flashed and she shook her head. "Cory's in the program. I don't want him to get kicked out if I…"

She thought he was flirting. Was he flirting? Hell yes, he was flirting.

He couldn't flirt with her. Bridget was coming soon. He wasn't this guy. The one who had one woman and started up with another.

You and Bridget aren't officially back together.

That didn't matter. He'd asked her to move to Jacksonville and it wasn't just so they could hang out occasionally and be friends. He wanted a wife and kids. He wanted it with someone he knew and was comfortable with. He owed it to Bridget to see if they could make things work. Not sabotage things with a bartender who had the face and body of an angel. A seductive angel… if seductive angels existed.

"No, I mean it's no big deal if we see each other." He managed a nonchalant shrug. "I believe you're not a stalker."

A second of confusion before her bubbly smile lit up her face and his afternoon. "Oh, good… I mean…great because I didn't want things to be weird." She waved her hand as if his words hadn't been the invitation they both knew they'd been. "Umm…well, thank you, I guess." She glanced at her watch. "You know, I'm late. Take care, okay?" She spun on her heel and sped up on her way to the door.

Isaiah watched her go. Nip the flirting in the bud. That was the right thing to do. He couldn't get tangled up with her. Even if the vision of his arms and legs tangled with

Angela's made his body get hotter than the heat wave they were currently in. No entanglements when he'd asked Bridget to move here with the intention of them getting back together. He turned and walked to the offices in the back to tell Keri he was leaving, but glanced over his shoulder at Angela's departing figure one more time.

Damn. Why did she have to be so fine?

Chapter 4

Angela half stumbled, half walked out of her bedroom while trying to slip her foot into one of the heels she wore at the bar. Neither Cory nor her neighbor, Nate, appeared to notice as she entered the living room. They were deep in conversation about Cory's first week of basketball camp and the greatness that was Isaiah Reynolds. For what seemed like the millionth time.

"Okay, enough about the Jacksonville Gators," Angela said. She pulled dangling silver earrings out of her pocket, flipped her hair over her shoulder and put one in her left ear.

Nate looked at her as if she was crazy. The muscle in his jaw worked as he chewed gum. "Why? I want to hear what's going on."

"For what? You aren't going to get any trade secrets about the team from what Cory sees at a summer camp." Angela put in the right earring.

"You don't know that."

Angela rolled her eyes. Nate may have been the twenty-seven-year-old owner of an office building in downtown Jacksonville that he'd had the brilliant idea of converting into a shared office space he leased to entrepreneurs who couldn't afford their own office areas, but when it came to the Gators, he was a kid. His toffee-colored eyes sparked with excitement and he'd actually put away the cell phone that seemed to be glued to his hand most of the time to talk with Cory about the Gators. Nate was a good friend, and an even better neighbor. Angela was eternally grateful he'd agreed to watch Cory some nights when she worked at the club.

"I do hear what's happening, Aunt Angela," Cory chimed in a tone that indicated he was "in the know" of all things Gators. "Isaiah says I have real talent. He told me that if I keep practicing, I have the potential to go far. He also said that the team is excited about their new recruits and hope to make it back to the playoffs this year. Did you know we'll get to visit the coliseum and tour the locker room?"

Nate sat forward in the chair. "Are you serious? If you need a chaperone for that, I can go with you."

Her heart fluttered every time she thought about the brief encounter with Isaiah at the center on Monday. Had he flirted with her, or had she misunderstood? All she could think about was how much she'd liked his touch. The seductive way he'd called her Angel. She was losing her mind! Which meant all talk of Isaiah needed to stop. It didn't help that he stopped to chat when she picked up Cory, or that sometimes their conversation still felt a little flirty.

She spun and went into the kitchen. She snatched a bag of marshmallows off the counter, stomped back into the living area and tossed the bag at Cory. "Here, eat those. Maybe that'll keep you from talking about the Gators for a second."

Cory's dark eyes brightened and he ripped into the bag. He grabbed three and shoved them into his mouth. "Thanks," he said around the wad of marshmallows.

Nate gave Angela a perplexed look. "Why do you want him to stop talking about the Gators? This is a great opportunity. Let the boy enjoy it."

"Yeah, Auntie, let me enjoy it," Cory mumbled.

She grabbed a small black-and-blue book bag from the chair and slipped it onto her shoulder. "I want you to enjoy camp. That doesn't mean I want to hear about it every second of the day."

Nate's eyebrows rose. "Why not?"

"Because she likes Isaiah and I think he likes her, too," Cory said with a mischievous grin before stuffing three more marshmallows into his mouth.

Nate's eyes widened. "Wait, what?"

Angela glared at her nephew. "Don't you have a princess to save in a video game or something?"

Cory shook his head. "No, but if you admit I'm old enough to stay here alone while you work, then I'll drop the subject."

Angela gritted her teeth. "Cory," she said in a warning tone. She was not having this argument again. She was new to this parenting thing, which meant he got a babysitter whether he liked it or not.

Cory's grin was filled with teenage manipulation. "I'm old enough."

"You're still a kid. A kid I'm responsible for." She pointed to his room. "Go save the princess."

Cory huffed and she waited for the argument, but his phone buzzed. He looked at it, then jumped up from the couch. "I gotta take this." He was down the hall and out of the room before she could ask who was on the phone.

Nate chewed gum and smirked. "You've got something going with Isaiah Reynolds?"

Angela wished she had another bag of marshmallows to throw. Dang teenagers and their big mouths. Cory was only in this camp for one month. She could avoid showing how much she wanted to swoon over Isaiah for one month.

She looked around for her keys. "What? No." The keys were on the end table next to the couch. She snatched them up.

Nate leaned back on the couch and crossed one ankle over the other knee. "Then why does Cory think something is going on?"

"He recognized me from the club." She looked toward the hall to make sure Cory wasn't coming back. Cory knew she was a bartender; he didn't know where she served drinks. "He came into Sweethearts after they won the championship."

Nate nodded his head as if everything suddenly made sense. "Ahh, so he's trying to get you in bed."

Angela slapped Nate's arm and laughed. "No, he's not."

Nate scooted away and shrugged. "That's what it sounds like to me."

"Regardless of what it sounds like, we can't hook up even if I wanted to. Cory would get kicked out of the camp and I'm not going to ruin his summer more than his parents already have."

She was Cory's support system for the summer. As much as the idea of being responsible for a teenager scared her, she wouldn't let fear keep her from doing her best to smooth out this rocky patch.

"You're not going to disappoint him," Nate said. "There aren't many people who would take in their brother's child without one word of complaint. I haven't heard you say a single negative thing since Heather dumped him on you."

Nor would she. Of course she was mad Heather

dropped off Cory and then hadn't called since, but the idea of Cory thinking she resented having him brought back her own ugly memories of her aunt's daily reminders of how much of a burden she and her brother were.

"He wasn't dumped on me. I'm his aunt and I can handle things. I'm not upset about having Cory here. I'm going to do everything I can to make sure he's happy and comfortable until his mom returns." *If* she returned. Heather hadn't set a definite return date. Her brother had four more years until she saw him.

"You aren't the least bit worried about what will happen if she isn't back before school starts?"

A cold sweat broke out over Angela's skin. She took a deep breath. No need to freak out about something that hadn't happened. "I got this," she said with a confidence that was a little shaky on her part. "I can handle whatever comes my way." She eyed the strength tattoo on her wrist and ran her finger over it. Her and one teenage boy for a few months. She could do this on her own.

Nate stood, wrapped an arm around her shoulder and gave her a side hug. "Nothing ever shakes Angela Bouler. I know you got this. You always handle your business."

Nate's confidence in her abilities overpowered her own doubts. "Which means I won't get him kicked out of camp just because Isaiah Reynolds might be interested in me."

"But if there was no camp issue, you'd want something to happen?"

A buzz of excitement tickled her. "I don't mess with the guys I meet at the club."

"Then why are you grinning from ear to ear?"

She forced the smile off her face. "I'm going to be late from work." Nate laughed and heat spread up Angela's neck and cheeks. "'Bye, Nate."

Nate chuckled and walked her to the door. "I'm just saying, when you hook up with Isaiah Reynolds, don't forget you've got friends that want tickets."

Angela waved him off. "Thanks again." She ignored his laughter as she went out the door.

Okay, so the idea of getting to know Isaiah Reynolds a little better wasn't terrible. She'd been interested that night they'd talked in the club, but he'd left without a backward glance. Then on Monday, when she'd bumped in to him, she'd thought he'd been flirting but he'd brushed off her assumption only to kinda flirt with her the rest of the week. Or maybe she just wanted to believe he was flirting. She couldn't get a read on him. Which made her feel silly for the way her pulse raced and her body buzzed when he'd touched her wrist. She was in the middle of a crush and he was looking at her as if she was just another random fan.

Maybe he didn't want to risk Cory's place in the camp, either?

If there wasn't the issue of Cory getting kicked out of camp, then she would flirt a little harder and put herself out there. She wasn't looking to get married and become dependent on a husband, but she didn't shy away from letting a guy know if she was interested. Cory wasn't going to be in camp forever. If she got the vibe again, she could drop the hint that after camp was over, she'd be willing to get to know him. After all, not going after the things she wanted wasn't in her personality. She'd gotten this far by trusting her instincts and every one of her instincts said Isaiah felt a little of what she felt, too.

Chapter 5

"I don't have to work tonight. Maybe we can try out that trampoline park?" Angela suggested to Cory while she walked him into camp.

Cory's annoyed sigh would have made disgruntled teens everywhere nod in approval. "I'm thirteen. I don't want to go to a trampoline park."

Angela gritted her teeth and counted to ten. The boy had been in a state all morning. He wouldn't tell her what was wrong, but the mood had grown over the weekend. Angela chalked it up to teenage mood swings.

She held open the door for Cory. "Fine. No trampolines. How about a movie?"

He dragged his feet through the door. "There's nothing out right now that I want to see."

Annoyance, meet my last nerve. "What do you want to do?"

"Nothing," he mumbled.

Angela couldn't suppress her sigh. *Try to remember what it was like to be thirteen and moody.* She remembered her aunt making Angela and Darryl feel like unwelcome houseguests the entire time. If anything, she worked harder to make Cory feel welcome in her tiny apartment, but damn, could he at least try to meet her halfway? She didn't know what to do when he just clammed up.

They walked in silence to the front desk and Angela smiled at the young man behind the counter, then signed in Cory for the day. She'd barely gotten her signature on the paper before Cory turned his back to her and stalked toward the opening of the gym.

"Cory." Angela dropped the pen on the desk and raised an eyebrow.

He sucked his teeth and grunted. "What?" He faced her with a glare.

"What?" *Oh, hell no.* Being patient with him was one thing, but letting him talk to her as if she was nothing was not about to happen.

She walked over, took his arm and pulled him away from the other arriving kids. "Look, I don't know what's gotten into you, but this attitude stops now. You do not snap at me and say 'what' like I'm some annoyance you're forced to deal with."

"You mean like I am to you?"

The retort slapped her in the chest. "What are you talking about? You're not an annoyance."

"But you're forced to deal with me. I know I'm a burden. You had your own life and I'm messing everything up."

Angela tried to keep up. Where had all of this come from? Last week he'd been happy about camp and teased her about liking Isaiah. Now he was angry and accusing her of not wanting him around? What could possibly have changed over a weekend?

She softened her voice. Concern replaced her anger. "No, you're not. You're my nephew and I love you."

"Before my dad went to jail I saw you about once a month—if that—and less than that after. Now I'm supposed to believe you're happy to have me in your apartment?"

Except for some holidays and birthdays she hadn't spent a lot of time with Cory before now. Only because Angela had always thought Heather was selfish—funny how her instincts has been right on that. It didn't mean she didn't love him. "I would do whatever it took to make sure you were with family instead of put in the system. You're not a burden. We're making things work."

"Well, maybe I don't want to make things work. I don't need my parents and I don't need your pity." He turned to walk away.

Angela took his arm and spun him to face her. "Where is all of this coming from? What's gotten into you?"

He jerked his arm away. "Just go to work, and leave me alone."

"Cory." Isaiah's stern voice broke into their argument. "Don't talk to your aunt like that."

Angela's heart imploded. Just what she needed—Isaiah witnessing how inadequate she was at dealing with teenage mood swings. She turned to him and wasn't too embarrassed to miss how good the green of his Gators T-shirt looked against his skin, as it draped over his muscular torso.

"I've got this," she said.

Isaiah looked from her to Cory's slumped shoulders. "I know, but I can't stand by and watch one of my camp kids be disrespectful. Cory, you need to apologize to your aunt."

Cory nudged his foot against the floor. "Sorry."

Isaiah crossed his arms over his chest. "The way you were disrespecting her was sorry. I need you to apologize. Like a man. Lift your chin and look her in the eye."

Cory raised his head and squared his shoulders. When

he met Angela's eye, there was a flash of regret. "I'm sorry, Auntie."

Angela placed her hand on his arm. He stiffened and glanced around. Several other kids from the camp watched. She squeezed his arm instead of pulling him into a hug. "Cory, I love you. You're not a burden and you're not unwelcome. I know we're still working things out, but we can't get through them if we don't work together. You can talk to me about anything. Don't forget that."

He nodded and the stiffness left his body. "I know." His gaze darted to the side. A young girl Angela recognized from the camp walked by on her way into the gym. Cory glanced back at Angela. "Can I go now?"

Angela nodded and dropped her hand. "We'll talk more later."

"Twenty laps," Isaiah said to Cory. "Learning to control your emotions is part of the discipline you'll need to be professional at anything. Think about that while you're running."

Cory sighed, but nodded and trudged into the gym. They both watched him go.

"What's going on with him today?" Isaiah asked.

Angela shrugged. She wished she knew where this burden nonsense came from, but Isaiah didn't need to know all her business. "He was in a bad mood when he woke up this morning, but it really started brewing over the weekend."

"He lives with you?" Isaiah's dark eyes met hers. She felt the force of his gaze like a blow to the stomach. It took her breath away. Without Cory there between them she was acutely aware of Isaiah's closeness. They didn't touch, but she could still *feel* him. His nearness was like an electric current in her vicinity. Powerful, potent and potentially dangerous.

She shifted away slightly. The distance didn't help. Isaiah was a big man and her instincts didn't want to escape his gravitational pull. "I'm his guardian for now. For the most part, things have been going really well. It's just when he gets like this…" *When I have no clue what I'm doing.* "I'm still learning the mind of a thirteen-year-old boy."

His shoulders relaxed and he arched an eyebrow. "You really don't want to know everything that goes on in the mind of a thirteen-year-old boy. Trust me." He chuckled. His laugh was low, warm and sexy.

"Is it that bad?"

Isaiah rubbed the back of his head and gave her a smile that had her sliding back into his circle. "Worse than you can imagine. I'll talk to him today and keep a close eye on him. He's a good kid, but I can tell he's got a lot going on in his head."

"You really don't have to do that. I'm not asking for any special treatment. Thanks for stepping in. I was about to go straight fool on him and that wouldn't have helped." She didn't like appearing as if she needed assistance, but she had to admit, Isaiah diffused Cory's sour attitude much faster than she had.

"It's no special treatment. When it comes to all of the kids in the camp, if I think one of them is struggling with something I talk to them. Sometimes it helps to talk things out with someone who isn't a parent."

"That's one of the reasons I thought he'd be willing to talk to me. I'm not his mom and he's never hesitated opening up to me before," Angela said, frowning.

"If he's staying with you, then he's probably viewing you as a mother figure."

Angela cringed and fought back panic. Mother figure. She reached for the diffuser charm she wore on a slim chain around her neck and inhaled the scent of lavender. She could do this. It was only for a summer.

"I guess you're right." She met Isaiah's eyes. He seemed to watch where her fingers toyed with the charm of her necklace in the V of her blouse. Angela dropped her hand. For several tense seconds, the air stuck in her lungs.

He quickly looked away. Angela tilted her head to the side. Was he blushing?

Before she could be sure, he ran a hand over his face and shrugged. "Because of that, he may be more comfortable talking with someone else."

"Someone like a famous basketball player whose memories of being thirteen will seem much cooler than mine."

Isaiah shoved a hand into the pocket of his black basketball shorts. "Believe me, my teenage memories are very boring. Chess-club member, anchor for the school morning-news show, the ugliest glasses you've ever seen. I was an official nerd. Far from considered cool."

Angela took in his tall, toned body and handsome face. For the life of her, she couldn't imagine him as a nerd. "You're joking."

"I'm dead serious. My younger brother and older sister were the cool ones. I was the geeky middle brother along for the ride. My dad put me in basketball when I was fourteen to help me get exercise. I ended up liking basketball more than chess. Some days, I still can't believe I made it to the pros."

She'd seen him play and couldn't imagine him not on the court. Finding out he hadn't always been a superconfident jock actually made sense. He was the "good guy" of the team. The one with the preppy bow ties and always in the news when the team did something in the community. She'd admired that about him. "There's nothing wrong with being a little nerdy."

"I didn't feel that way then. Girls did not look my way." His voice didn't hold any hint of lingering resentment, but just enough self-deprecation to make her chuckle.

"If they'd known you'd grow into such a fine man they wouldn't have ignored you."

He rubbed the back of his neck and glanced away. The hint of red appeared beneath his pecan skin, which in turned made him even cuter.

"That's the thing," he said. "I wouldn't want them to like me because they knew I was going to be a professional baller. I'd rather they liked me because I was me."

"I'm sure there were other girls like me, who tended to crush on the smart guys in class. I don't like brashness and bravado. I prefer someone more laid-back. Someone I can talk to all night about anything and everything."

Like they'd talked the night he'd sat at her bar for hours. He hadn't been interested in the women onstage, hadn't drooled down the front of her shirt, or spent the entire time trying to get her to go home with him. He'd talked to her about movies, music, the right way to make a martini. She hadn't truly enjoyed talking to a guy in a long time.

"Yeah, I like that, too." His gaze probed hers. His pull made her want to reach out to him. Run her hands across the strength of his chest. Run her lips over the fullness of his.

Movement in the corner of her eye drew her attention. Keri smiled but there was a sharpness in her eyes as she walked over that made Angela step back from Isaiah.

"Everything good?" Keri asked, and when she looked at Angela her eyebrows drew slightly together.

If Cory had guessed there was a vibe between her and Isaiah after a few seconds, then she shouldn't be surprised Keri would look concerned after she and Isaiah had been speaking for several minutes.

Angela acknowledged Keri's concern with a nod. "Everything is fine. Isaiah stepped in with Cory this morning. He's in a bit of a mood." She smiled at Isaiah. "Thanks again. I better get to work."

Isaiah tilted his head forward. The slight bow would have looked silly if another man had done it, but seemed fitting when Isaiah made the motion. "You're more than welcome."

Keri shifted next to Angela. Angela tore her gaze from Isaiah, said a quick goodbye to Keri and got out of there before she forgot that succumbing to Isaiah's pull right now had consequences that would affect Cory. Three more weeks of camp and then maybe she'd be able to find out if he was into her, too. Angela smiled on her way to the car.

Isaiah watched Cory as he stared with all the longing of a teen in love. The target of his longing was Denise, one of the girls in the camp. Cory sat alone on the bleachers during the lunch break, watching Denise but never gathering the courage to walk over to speak to her. Cory's crush on the girl was obvious, but if she looked his way, he stammered and walked away. All of his bravado on the court evaporated when Denise smiled at him.

Isaiah could relate to the boy's struggle. He'd felt the same way when he was a teen. Felt that way now whenever Angela smiled at him. Just like an angel, the brightness of her smile struck him speechless. She must think he was ridiculous.

He'd blushed! What the hell. Kevin would take his man card if he knew.

"What are you frowning about?" his teammate Will Hampton asked.

Will sat next to Isaiah on the bleachers. He was taller than Isaiah at six foot six, with dark skin, a full beard and dark eyes that were always sparkling with laughter. Will lived life with an enthusiasm that tended to spill over to everyone around him. That's why he was one of the most popular members on the team.

Isaiah pointed toward Cory across the gym. "Cory is too afraid to go over and speak to Denise."

Will followed Isaiah's gaze. "He has been giving her puppy-dog eyes from day one."

"Thing is, she's been giving him the same puppy-dog eyes. I think she would respond well if he decided to talk to her."

"Then he should talk to her," Will said with the confidence of a guy who'd never been afraid to approach a woman he was interested in. Isaiah couldn't quite call Will a player because even though he always had a new woman on his arm, he always ended up their friend and was yet to have one of his flings get possessive or clingy with him. Isaiah had no idea how the man did that.

"You don't know how hard it is to go up to a girl. I used to be petrified to talk to girls I liked when I was that age."

Will grinned and slapped Isaiah on the back. "That's because you were overthinking things. Women are easy. You smile, tell them they have nice eyes and before you know it, they're giggling and eating up everything you're spitting. Treat them with respect when you're ready to move on, or make them think it's their idea that they're ending things and you're golden."

"Shut up," Isaiah said without any heat. "The world already knows you wiggle your finger and women come flocking."

Will laughed and tugged on his collar. "Hey, I've got a gift."

Isaiah looked at Cory again. Angela had said he didn't have to talk to Cory, but he wanted to know why the boy had been so rude to his aunt. Maybe it was something as simple as pining over a girl he liked. Isaiah stood. "I'll go talk to him. He was giving his aunt a hard time earlier today. There may be a few things on his mind."

"Isn't his aunt that bartender at Sweethearts?" Will's voice rose in interest.

"Yes." Isaiah's tone hardened. He gave Will a hard look.

Will only smiled and leaned back. "I thought so. You two talked for a long time the night we were all out."

"And?"

"And is she the reason why you're so concerned about Cory?"

Isaiah would have stepped in if any of the kids at camp had disrespected their parent or guardian in his vicinity. Yet, he couldn't deny something else made him especially want to lend a helping hand in this case. "I'd help out no matter what and you know that. His aunt has nothing to do with this."

"Uh-huh." Will's tone called Isaiah a liar.

"Bridget is coming to town in a few days. I'm not that kind of guy."

Will's smile grew. "Uh-huh."

Isaiah ignored the teasing glint in Will's eye and waved him off. He hopped down the bleachers and crossed the gym to Cory. Cory appeared to notice him, sitting up straighter and trying to look relaxed.

"I'm not doing anything," he said.

Isaiah sat next to the kid. "I'm not going to give you a hard time. I just want to talk."

"Everyone wants to talk," Cory mumbled. He pulled on a shoestring and scowled.

"That's because we care about how you're feeling. If we didn't care, we wouldn't want to know what's going on."

Cory cocked his head in Isaiah's direction. "We?" He sounded confused.

"Me and your aunt. You were giving her a hard time earlier today."

Cory went back to pulling his shoestring. "I didn't mean to."

Isaiah tapped the boy's side so that he'd look at him. "Then why were you?"

Cory dropped the shoestring and sat up. "She's trying too hard," he said in a rush.

"Trying too hard?"

Cory pulled on his fingers in a frustrated motion. "To act like I'm not a problem for her when I know I am. She's treating me like I'm a little kid. Like she can't be real with me. She just acts like everything is okay and when I offer to help she tells me to go play video games or something."

"And that hit you this morning so you had to be rude to her?" Isaiah didn't buy it. Something else had to be going on.

Cory frowned. "The other night I asked her if I could stay home by myself while she worked. I'm thirteen now. Most thirteen-year-olds stay home. Instead, she gets her friend Nate to *babysit* me every night she works late." Cory said *babysit* as if it was an act of the highest treason.

A knot formed in Isaiah's stomach. "Nate? Is that her boyfriend?"

Cory shook his head. "No, he lives next door and they're friends. You don't have to worry."

"Why would I worry?"

Cory just gave Isaiah a look that said *whatever.* "Anyway, I know I'm a burden, but she's trying too hard to make me think I'm not."

Isaiah forced away thoughts of the nonboyfriend Nate and focused on Cory's problem. "Maybe Angela doesn't want to burden you with her problems. She's the adult, you're the kid." When Cory glared, Isaiah held up a hand. "Last time I checked thirteen was still a minor. There's nothing wrong with her not wanting to upset you."

"But I know me being there is a problem. She dropped out of school for the summer because of me. She can't work her extra job because of me. She had to accept the charity that sent me to this camp. Add to that, she's always trying to act like everything is cool. Like taking me to a movie or a trampoline park."

"What's wrong with making you happy?" Isaiah leaned forward and rested his elbows on his knees. He turned his head to look at Cory. The boy seemed so downcast he wasn't sure if anything he said would make him feel better, but he had to try. "If your aunt didn't want you there, I'm pretty sure you would know it. If she's trying to make you feel comfortable, that's a good thing. It means she loves you and she wants you to be happy. I'm pretty sure this is her first crack at taking care of a teenager. She's got to get used to you just like you have to get used to her. Maybe think about that whenever you're feeling frustrated. And don't freak out over the babysitter thing. Once she feels confident you can take care of yourself, I'm sure she'll let you stay home alone while she works."

Cory's lips pursed and his brow furrowed while he thought about that. Finally he said, "I just don't want her to decide I'm not worth it and kick me out."

"Then you may want to cut back on the attitude and not get angry when she's trying." Cory looked a little sick, so Isaiah reached over and playfully hit his shoulders. "Don't worry. I doubt your aunt will kick you out. Seems like she kinda likes you."

Cory relaxed and smiled. "Yeah…she's cool. When she's not trying to not make me feel like a baby."

"So, take it easy on her. Just a little."

"I will." Cory looked across the gym. His body stiffened.

Isaiah followed his gaze. Another kid in camp, a boy named Kirk, had walked over to talk with Denise and her friends. Kirk was more outspoken than Cory and that had made him one of the instantly popular kids in the camp.

"You know," Isaiah said slowly, "when I was your age, I was afraid to talk to a girl I liked."

Cory glanced at Isaiah out of the corner of his eye. "Really?"

Isaiah nodded and felt a little flattered by the disbelief in the boy's tone. He guessed he really didn't resemble the awkward kid he used to be, even if he still felt that way at times. "Yes."

"When did it get easier for you to talk to girls?"

"Who said it got easier?" Isaiah said. "I just had to learn that nine times out of ten, if I was respectful and just approached her with no hidden agenda, she would at least listen to what I had to say."

"You mean she didn't laugh at you? Because, girls will

laugh at you now if they think you're being corny. Things are different from the way they were back in your day."

Isaiah winced and put a hand over his chest as if wounded. "My day wasn't that long ago." Cory rolled his eyes, a gesture Isaiah decided to ignore. Everyone over twenty seemed old when you were thirteen. "All I'm saying is, if you like a girl, just talk to her. You don't have ask her to be your girlfriend or anything like that. If she likes basketball…talk to her about that."

Cory sat up straighter and watched Denise and Kirk. Denise had just turned her back to the other boy, which meant Cory probably didn't have to worry about him as a potential rival. "What should I say about basketball?"

"Start with 'hey,' then ask her who her favorite ball-player is."

Cory looked at Isaiah. "Why would I ask a girl that?"

"Because you like Denise and if she's in a basketball camp, then she probably has a favorite basketball player. Don't worry. She sneaks looks at you, too."

Cory's face brightened up. "She does?" His deepening voice momentarily returned to the squeak of childhood.

Isaiah fought back a smile. He didn't want Cory to think he was teasing him. "She does. Just walk over and say 'hey.'"

"Even with Kirk and her friends over there?"

"Especially with Kirk over there. Don't show her you're intimidated by another man. Girls don't like that."

Cory nodded and watched Denise and Kirk. "Don't be intimidated." He took a deep breath and stood. He shook out his hands and shoulders, then jumped down the bleachers. He looked back at Isaiah over his shoulders. "Oh, and Mr. Isaiah?"

"Yeah."

"Auntie looks at you, too. So, you know, if you like

her, you can just talk to her." Cory smiled, then strode across the room with a show of confidence that impressed Isaiah.

Isaiah leaned back on the bleachers. *So Auntie Angel looks at me.* A smile broke across his face. He shouldn't care. Bridget was coming. That's who should be on his mind, but that wasn't what kept his mood up for the rest of the day.

Chapter 6

Angela arrived at the center well before five thirty. Everything had worked out for her at the end of the day. No issues with volunteers, but her boss had called a meeting to talk about possible late hours due to a group coming in to cross-train from another state. The idea of another change to her already packed schedule made her cringe, but until the change actually happened, she wouldn't worry.

Angela entered the center and found Keri at the front desk. "Hey, what are you doing up here?" Keri was usually running around handling more important things while the teenage workers and volunteers handled signing the kids in and out for the day.

"Just covering for one of my guys while he cleans up something in one of the classrooms." Keri said with a smile.

Angela was happy to see her wary expression from earlier today, when she'd interrupted Angela's conversation with Isaiah, was gone. She didn't want Keri to have a reason to question Cory's participation in the camp.

"How did Cory do today?" Angela asked as she signed her name and the pickup time beside Cory's name in the notebook. "He was in kind of a mood this morning."

Keri shook her head. "No problems at all. All of the players think he's doing a really great job."

Relief washed over her. She's spent the day worrying about Cory. She still had no idea what had put him in such a bad mood earlier that day. She didn't know the best way to get him to confess without sounding like a nag. Was she supposed to nag? This entire parenting thing was so new to her. She wanted to do the right thing, but knowing what was the right thing was harder than she'd expected. "Good to hear. Well, I'll go get him."

Keri nodded and Angela walked to the gym. She took Keri's statement that Cory had a good day to mean whatever had been bothering him was no longer a factor—unless she was the problem. Sure, she'd argued with him about staying home alone, but that was because she'd never forgive herself if something happened to Cory while she worked nights at the club. Eventually she'd have to trust him. He would be fourteen later this summer. Nate couldn't always babysit and she'd be damned if she called her aunt to help. As much as she worried, she had to face the fact that she was playing single parent right now and would have to trust Cory alone no matter how much the idea scared her.

Cory wasn't in the gym. She asked one of the camp volunteers and was directed down a hallway, where Cory was apparently helping to put away the basketballs. When she found the storage room, another counselor told her Cory had gone to the locker room with another kid. To that point, she would've waited for him in the lobby, but she didn't doubt Cory would take his time talking in the locker room and she'd be twiddling her thumbs forever.

She stopped outside the boys' locker room and pushed the door slightly open. "Cory, you in there?" she called without going in. The last thing she wanted was to freak out a bunch of boys by entering their domain.

The sound of a locker slamming shut and the echo of music was her only answer. The song was one Cory listened to constantly. Something about a girl being a crowd pleaser. There weren't a bunch of voices raised in conversation. Which meant if Cory was in there, he wasn't with a group of kids and probably hadn't heard her over the music.

Angela glanced down the hall, took a deep breath and shielded her eyes as she stepped into the locker room. "Come on, Cory, we've got to go."

She rounded the corner and stopped just short of bumping into Isaiah yet again. He held out a hand to stop her from colliding with him. He was in the same athletic shirt and basketball shorts from earlier and had a duffel bag over one shoulder. Almost running into him had brought her dangerously close to his body. She was so close her knees turned to Vaseline and her heart decided now was a damn good time to flutter.

"Oh, I'm so sorry," Angela said, flustered. Being close to him short-circuited her brain. She wanted to run away and run her hands over his body all at the same time. "I'm looking for Cory. Someone said he was in here. When I heard the song, I thought…"

Isaiah tapped the screen of the phone in his hand and the song stopped. "He's out back near the walking track. One of the volunteers needed help bringing in equipment and he volunteered after helping me straighten up the locker room."

Angela nodded and tried to pretend the effort to not run her gaze over his body from head to toe wasn't harder than a pack-a-day smoker quitting cold turkey. She took a step back. "Thanks. I'll see you later."

"Before you go…" Isaiah met her gaze, stilled, blinked, then lowered his eyes to his phone. He sucked in a breath before looking at her again. "I had a talk with Cory earlier today."

"You didn't have to do that." The denial of assistance was automatic.

The corner of Isaiah's sexy mouth lifted in a half smile that made her believe he'd expected her to say that. "I know, but he was upset about something. I didn't want that to distract him from what we're working on in camp."

Her curiosity and concern for Cory overruled her need to tell him not to get involved. "Did he tell you what was wrong?"

Isaiah put the duffel bag on one of the benches. He lifted his foot to the bench and leaned his forearm on his thigh. The pose was casual enough, but it made not checking out the play of muscles in his long legs, nor focusing on the impressive bulge between his legs, pretty much impossible. Angela lifted her chin and trained her gaze on his chin. If she looked him in the eye she couldn't guarantee he wouldn't see where her thoughts had gone. If she dropped her gaze…she'd be drooling.

"He feels you treat him like a baby, but he's also worried about being a burden to you."

"What? I don't treat him like a baby." That got her attention off of inappropriate things. Sure, she wasn't ready to let him stay home alone, but that's because he was still a kid. She'd give all her savings to find out where the burden idea had come from? She'd done everything she could to make Cory feel welcome. She didn't want him to be as uncomfortable in her house as she'd felt with her aunt.

"He thinks he's old enough to stay home alone, but I understand why you would hesitate. Honestly, I think his real issue is that he doesn't know how to help out. He said you're trying very hard to make him comfortable, but he knows you've given up a lot for him."

"I never once said anything to him about that."

Isaiah placed his hand on her arm. It was a comforting gesture that also made her very aware of the softness of his fingertips against her skin. "He didn't say you had. He's afraid you're hiding how you really feel and one day you'll snap and kick him out."

Angela sank onto the bench. Her purse hit the floor with a thud. "Of course I would never kick him out. Crap, I don't know what I'm doing."

Isaiah dropped his foot, straddling the bench to face her. "I didn't mean to upset you. I just thought you'd want to know."

Angela took a deep breath and ran her fingers through her hair. "I do. It's just so difficult. This situation with Cory is new for both of us. I never expected to be a parent. Now I've got a thirteen-year-old boy to watch out for."

"Boys are easy. Feed him, listen when he decides to talk and don't press him too hard."

Obviously it wasn't that easy if Cory worried she'd kick him out one day. What had she done wrong? Had she unconsciously shown him how hard a time she was having in adjusting? Her stomach twisted. "No matter how much of a challenge this is, I would never kick him out. He's not a burden and I don't want him to think he is. My aunt took me in at thirteen and she made life miserable for me and my brother—Cory's dad. I'm not like her." The words came out with a vehemence she felt deep in her soul. No way would she allow herself to become as cruel as her aunt had been.

"How long will Cory be with you? Is your brother—"

"My brother is in jail."

She wasn't looking at him but she felt his discomfort. Saw the way he reached for her, then pulled back. "I'm sorry."

"Don't be. That's what happens when you think you are some type of big-shot embezzler, but you're really just a petty thief. Cory's mom is in New York trying her hand at a career on the stage. She said Cory would be in the way and dropped him off with me."

"You took him in without hesitation?"

Her gaze lifted to his. "Of course. He's my nephew. No one deserves to feel unwanted."

He didn't look as if he doubted her. If anything, the light in his eyes said her quick reply impressed him. "Maybe just chill a little. He appreciates you, but he can sense if you're trying too hard to be happy. That in turn makes him feel like a little kid that can't do anything to help. If he's like I was, he's going to want to help where he can. Let him see that you're trying to make him comfortable, but be real when things get tough. When he tries to step in and help, if it makes sense, let him. You guys are a team right now."

Isaiah was right. She wasn't used to accepting help, but when she'd been in the similar situation she'd wanted to help her aunt out. To try to be as good as she could to keep her aunt from yelling and accusing them of making her life miserable. Though she'd never be that cruel to Cory, he probably wanted to lessen any feelings he had of imposing on her just the same.

"I'll think about what you said. I am trying hard to not make Cory uncomfortable. Has everything been easy since he moved in? No, but I won't let him know that. I try to focus on the good in a situation. Complaining changes nothing and helps no one."

"Another sign of your strength." His gaze lowered to her wrist.

Angela glanced down at the tattoo there. The symbol for strength she'd gotten after getting through her first year of undergraduate studies. "You remembered what this stands for?" She turned her hand over until her wrist faced up and ran the fingers of her other hand over the symbol.

"I'm not likely to forget. That night we talked, you seemed really proud of the tattoo. I could tell in your voice you're not a woman likely to succumb to weakness." His dark eyes met hers and her insides quivered like a dozen newly emerged butterflies. "That's a really admirable trait."

The heat from a blush started in her chest and crept up to her cheeks. She tucked her hair behind her ear and looked back at her tattoo. His gaze stayed on her. She wanted to squirm, or wiggle closer to him. Time to get out of there.

"Thanks for talking to him and telling me," she said. She hated interference, but he'd given her good insight on what was happening with Cory. For that, she couldn't be upset.

She moved to get up and Isaiah placed his fingertips on her arm. The touch was light, but she felt it all the way to her small toe. The man sent electric currents through her whenever they touched.

"There was another thing," he said. He pulled his hand back quickly.

She still felt the light imprint of his touch on her arm. "What?"

"He likes a girl here at camp. I think that was bothering him, too."

"Girl trouble, too." She was completely unprepared to

give him advice when it came to a girl. She didn't want to imagine that he was ready for that. Imagining meant acknowledging she had a thirteen-year-old with raging hormones in her house and all that came with it.

She must have made a look because Isaiah held up a hand as if to tell her not to freak out. "Don't worry, I talked to him about that, too. I gave him a little advice."

"What advice did you give him?"

"Basic advice. I told him that if you like a girl, then talk to her. Tell her how you feel. Don't hide in the corner because she's sure to ignore you."

She relaxed a little. That wasn't too bad. Not that she should have expected him to tell Cory something asinine. He was the good guy of the team. "Is that what you do? Tell a woman when you like her?"

"It is." He glanced at her tattoo. Slowly brought his gaze up her body to meet hers. Angela's body reacted as if she'd been caressed. "For instance, I like you."

Her lips parted. Her heart did a now-or-never tango in her chest. She'd wondered if she'd just imagined the vibe between them. Those three simple words plus the intense look in his eyes gave her the answer. A giddy excitement of knowing the guy she'd been crushing on felt the same made her feel like she was soaring. Isaiah seemed to focus on her parted lips. His eyes darkened with a promise of passion. He swallowed hard and shifted on the bench. If she didn't know better, she'd think he was nervous or unsure. Which was kind of cute.

"I like you, too," she whispered.

Isaiah ran his hands over his thighs. He cleared his throat. "I should—"

Angela leaned in and brushed her lips over his before she lost her nerve. One kiss, that's all she wanted. She wasn't one to be shy about things and if he was unsure, she didn't want him to think she wasn't interested. Three weeks until the camp ended and she didn't want to have a what-if thought in her head when she was actually free to see if the connection they'd started that night at the bar was real.

She'd intended to make the kiss brief. Just to let him know she was interested. But his hand cupped the side of her face right before she would have pulled away. Angela leaned farther into him. Isaiah's other arm wrapped around her waist and pulled her closer. His head slanted and he kissed her deeply. Not a hard, demanding kiss, but a definite answer to her softer question. His lips and tongue played across her mouth, causing her to crave more with each pass. She gripped his upper arm and pressed closer to him. She wanted to twist her position and straddle his hips.

If she did that in this skirt, they'd be screwed...or screwing.

Her hand rested on the hard muscle of his thigh. She squeezed and was seduced by the power vibrating through his tense muscles. His slow tasting turned into a more insistent kiss, robbing her of breath and leaving her with no choice but to be lost in the delicious pleasure of his lips on hers.

Voices near the door. They jerked apart, their breathing hard and heavy. The voices trailed away. He licked his lips. Angela groaned and took stock of how completely he'd turned her body into a throbbing nerve of desire, her nipples hard and aching, panties damp, breathing uncontrollable. If she didn't leave she would straddle his hips and slide him right into the spot that longed for attention.

"I've got to find Cory." Her voice was a husky whisper.

He nodded. "You should."

Unease crept through her. Was he ashamed or upset

by what happened? She stood on shaky legs. Isaiah took her hand in his. When he met her eyes she gasped. Raw hunger reflected in his gaze. He squeezed her hand, then let it go.

Angela bit her lip to keep from smiling. She nodded and hurried out of the locker room. Thankfully no one was there to question her. She wouldn't have been able to come up with a good excuse. Isaiah Reynolds had kissed her. And based on the look he'd just given her, it wouldn't be the last time. The very idea made her heart soar.

Chapter 7

Isaiah called Bridget as soon as he got out of the shower after arriving home. He needed to solidify his resolve. He'd thought of Angela nonstop since kissing her. Her sparkling brown eyes, heart-stopping smile, captivating curves and seductive voice. Everything about her tempted him. Temptation wasn't what he needed. Stability, trust and mutual respect born from friendship—those were the things that made relationships last. Sure, he could sleep with Angela—he could *really* sleep with her—but that would ruin the strong foundation he had with Bridget.

He sat on the massive king-size bed in the bedroom of his home and waited for Bridget to pick up.

"Isaiah, hey." Bridget's voice was cordial but confused. Voices in the background made hearing her difficult.

"Did I catch you at a bad time?"

"No. I'm out with some friends. We're celebrating the end of school. They wanted to wish me well before I embark on the next chapter in my life. Is everything all right?"

Isaiah leaned forward and rested his elbow on his thigh. "Everything is good. I just wanted to talk to you."

"About what?"

He let out an incredulous laugh. "About nothing. Just to talk."

"Oh." There was a pause. The conversation of her friends in the background was the only response.

"Is that a problem?" Was he wrong to feel a little uneasy by her lack of a response? Maybe he was just looking for trouble where there wasn't any.

"No, um…hang on a second. Let me walk away from the group."

He waited a few minutes while the muffled voices of her talking to her friends came through. Things quieted down and he guessed she'd either left the restaurant or found a quiet spot.

"Are you sure everything is okay?" she asked when she returned to the phone.

"Why wouldn't it be okay? I've called you to talk before."

"I know. I'm just making sure."

Did he need a reason to call her now? He had just asked her to move to his city. "So you're celebrating the next step."

"Yeah. They're all really happy for me." Excitement entered her voice.

Isaiah perked up. Excitement was good. "Are you as happy as they are?"

"Of course. I didn't expect things to turn out so well."

"I always figured this was how things would work out." When they'd taken the break before her last year of law school it had been with the understanding they would see how things felt once she finished. She'd told him then she couldn't imagine spending her life with anyone else.

"You did? Because I had my doubts," Bridget said.

"Why would you have doubts?"

Isaiah hadn't *burned* to have her back the way Kevin

thought he should, and he had casually dated one other woman in the year since they split, but he'd always known when he settled down, he'd go back to Bridget. She knew him. He didn't feel flustered or out of control when he was with her. Their families got along great. They made sense.

"Because, Goldman Schultz is one of the top firms in northern Florida," Bridget said in a voice that indicated she hadn't been thinking about their relationship at all. "They represent the interests of a lot of high-profile and substantial businesses in the area. Even with my GPA and family name, I wasn't sure they'd take a chance on me."

Isaiah's resolve flopped harder than an opponent trying to force a foul. "You're talking about Goldman Schultz?"

"Yes. I told you they offered me a job."

"You told me you applied and interviewed, but I didn't know you had it."

"Oh…well that's why we're celebrating. What were you talking about?" She really sounded confused.

"You moving here." He hesitated a second. "Us getting back together."

"Oh, right. Of course I'm happy about that, too." She laughed but it sounded forced. "I mean, our parents practically have us married already."

Doubt slithered into his brain. "If you hadn't landed the job with Goldman Schultz, would you still have come to Jacksonville?"

There was a moment of silence that was a shade too long. "Yes. I would have at least considered coming."

"At least considered."

"Come on, Isaiah. We both knew how hard it was for us to work out when we weren't in the same city. If I hadn't gotten the job, us getting back together would have been unreasonable. Neither of us like long-distance."

She was right. They wouldn't work if she lived elsewhere. "What if there was no job here and I still wanted you to move so we could get back together?"

"I don't—"

A woman's voice interrupted. "Come on, Bridget. They're bringing your cake out."

"Okay, I'm coming right now. Look, Isaiah, let's talk about this later when I'm in town."

He ran a hand over his face. "See you next week."

"See you soon. Can't wait. 'Bye." The words were automatic and held a hint of relief.

He stared at the dark phone screen. Well, that hadn't gone as he expected. Being unsure wasn't supposed to be a part of his relationship with Bridget. His brain said this was the right move, but something about the decision still felt…off. One conversation didn't mean he should start up anything with another woman. Bridget would be there next week. Maybe things would be different when he saw her again versus talking on the phone. He would work out his feelings for her before doing anything else. Rash decisions lead to rash actions, like chaining himself to a fence to save the home of a girl. That rash action had cost him his first college scholarship offer and nearly cost his parents their jobs at the university. No more rash decisions for him in life or love.

He stood and strode to the kitchen for something to drink, satisfied he would trust his judgment over his hormones. Though he still wondered what Angela was doing now.

Chapter 8

Angela slid a drink across the bar. The man barely threw her a glance. His eyes were glued to the woman dancing on the stage.

"Enjoy the show, sir," she said in an encouraging tone.

She looked at the two other men at the bar to see if they needed anything, but they too were captivated by the dancer. Getting ignored because of the dancers was the ultimate goal. The Thursday-night crowd was decent. Thursday night was half-off wings-and-beer night, which meant a bigger crowd going into the start of the weekend. All the guys at the bar seemed satisfied, so she decided to enjoy the breathing room. There were a few drink orders from the waitresses serving customers on the floor so she got to work on those.

"Why in the hell are you humming?" a female voice said from behind Angela.

Angela glanced over her shoulder at her friend and one of the dancers, Vicki. Onstage, Vicki went by the name Honey, and played up the name by wearing a sexy bear costume that consisted of a faux-fur bra and skirt that barely covered her behind. Glitter body oil made her brown skin shimmer in the lights of the club, and long blond highlighted hair hung loose around her slim shoulders. Every dancer, waitress and bartender at Sweethearts wore something to play up their stage names. Angela became Angel and always wore sparkly white wings with her tank top and skirts.

"I'm not humming," Angela said before concentrating on the rum and Coke she was making.

"I can hear you humming over the music." Vicki leaned against the bar next to Angela. Her whiskey-colored gaze analyzed Angela from head to toe. "And you're grinning. What gives?"

"Why are you over here? Aren't you next onstage?" Angela asked without any heat. Vicki always came over to chat during the night, but until her friend pointed it out, Angela hadn't realized she had been humming and smiling. Cupid had definitely speared her with one of his arrows.

"Sapphire just started, and based on the amount of money being tossed onstage, I'll be lucky to get pennies after she's done." There wasn't a lick of hate in Vicki's tone. There was still plenty of money to be made and Honey never failed to have guys reaching deep into their pockets.

One of the waitresses came over and Angela put the drinks she'd prepared on her tray. After she walked away, Angela faced Vicki.

"So, go ahead and tell me. Why are you humming? Is it a man?" Vicki twirled a lock of hair around her finger and eagerly watched Angela.

"Why does it have to be a man?"

"And you must like him a lot." Vicki pointed at Angela and bounced on her toes. "You're blushing and trying not to grin from ear to ear. You're crazy about him."

Angela put a hand on her hip. "Am I that easy to read?"

"Yes. Now tell me who he is."

Angela glanced at the men sitting at the bar. None of them paid her or Vicki any attention. "You wouldn't believe me if I told you."

Vicki slid close. "Now I've got to know."

"You're going to think I'm crazy." Angela thought the entire situation was crazy.

Vicki rubbed her hands together. "Finally, you've got something juicy in your love life. I can't be the only one with a story."

"My situation is nowhere near as intriguing as yours." Vicki was sneaking around with one of the bouncers named Bruno. Their boss, Z, had a strict policy of no fraternizing between employees. Vicki and Bruno had been seeing each other on the sly for almost a year. Which meant Angela had spent the last year living vicariously through Vicki and her we-almost-got-caught-in-the-dressing-room stories.

Vicki raised a shoulder and batted her eyes in an exaggerated fashion. "What can I say, the forbidden excites me." The both laughed.

Work and school had kept Angela's dating life to a few coffee dates that weren't worth progressing to lunch, never mind dinner. Listening to Vicki's stories made her yearn for her own illicit encounter. The memory of Isaiah's hard, hot body next to hers. The hum of desire vibrating below the surface when they'd kissed. The I'm-going-to-explode-if-I-don't-touch-him feeling right before they'd kissed.

"I can understand the temptation of wanting what you shouldn't have," Angela said breathlessly.

Vicki's eyes widened. "Okay, start talking right now. No one is paying us any damn attention. Go."

Angela laughed at Vicki's customary direct nature.

"You remember when the Gators came in after their championship win?"

"Yeah, and you spent all night talking to the preppy one at the bar."

Angela nodded but didn't say anything more. Vicki's jaw dropped. Her hand covered her mouth. "You and the preppy one?"

Vicki was the closest thing to a sister Angela had and the words spilled out of her. "Cory is in the camp they put on every summer. He recognized me. The vibe is still there."

"So you're hooking up?"

"We can't. If we hook up, Cory's out of the program." A new drink order printed on the bar printer. "But I think he likes me."

"Okay, tell me what he did and I'll tell you if he likes you."

"He kissed me. Well, I kissed him. But my kiss was real quick and then he really kissed me back." Her body flushed.

Vicki slapped Angela's arm. "Yeah, chick, I think he likes you."

"I know. Which is crazy, right? It has to be crazy. Guys like that don't come in places like this and really fall for us."

Vicki rolled her eyes. "Says who? Hollywood or some backward ideology of who deserves to be happy? We aren't doing anything wrong and we aren't hurting anyone. We have just as much right to have a dream man as any corporate lawyer."

"I know that, but this is real life. What if I can't trust him?"

Vicki's eyes softened. "Trust yourself. If he seems like a creep only out to get some, then move on. If not, seriously, why would you not take a chance with a professional baller? Even if he is the preppy one."

Angela poured shots of tequila. "There's nothing wrong with being the preppy one."

"True. The good guys always fall in love fast and hard," Vicki said thoughtfully. Her eyes widened again. "You could be on the next reality show with athlete wives."

Angela held up a hand to stop her friend. "No one's talking about love or marriage. I've worked too hard to get my degree and take care of myself to give it up to become some baller's trophy wife. I'm just thinking we might date for a few months and even in that time, I'm not planning on taking his money."

"Why not?"

"Because when it's over I don't want to owe him anything. I won't be dependent on anyone but me. I like Isaiah, and if the vibe is still there when camp is over, I'm willing to date him after Cory finishes the program."

Vicki crossed her arms and pouted. "Only you would hesitate at the chance of being a baller's wife. You know half the women in here would be setting the trap to land him for life."

Angela placed the shots on a tray for the waitress and chuckled. "I'm not half the women in here. I'm me." And she'd worked too hard to stand on her own feet to entertain the idea of giving control to anyone else.

Chapter 9

She'd kissed him.

He'd kissed her back.

Damn! The kiss had been good. Great. Not enough.

A week later and he couldn't stop thinking about her lips, so soft and delicious. The slight weight of her curves barely pressed against his body. The struggle to not lift and turn her until she straddled him, not run his fingers through the thick softness of her hair and not press his dick into the heat at the juncture of her thighs, was very real.

"When does Bridget come to town?" Kevin's voice broke into Isaiah's thoughts.

Isaiah blinked and slightly shook his head. He glanced around at the camp kids as they took dozens of pictures in the Gators' locker room. His focus was on hiatus today. Instead of making sure the kids were enjoying their tour of the stadium, he was still thinking about a kiss that shouldn't have happened in the first place.

"Tomorrow," Isaiah said. "She's supposed to be in town by the time I'm finished with camp."

Exactly why he shouldn't be thinking about Angela's kiss. He had to talk to Angela and apologize for kissing her. But the idea of saying the kiss was wrong seemed ridiculous.

Nothing that good could be wrong.

Yet, kissing her back, especially like that, had been wrong. Bridget was on her way. He couldn't break things off with her before they'd even started just because he was attracted to Angela. Could he?

"No offense, but you don't seem that excited," Kevin said.

Kevin was dressed casually for the tour in a yellow T-shirt and camouflage cargo pants. The kids had gotten a kick out of asking about Kevin's tattoos. Especially the newest one of the championship trophy on his right forearm. Thank goodness Kevin was focused on what they were supposed to be doing.

Isaiah tugged on the collar of his navy-and-white-striped shirt. "I'm looking forward to seeing her."

"Why don't you sound convincing?"

Isaiah knew why; it was because he wasn't convinced. Keri announced it was time for the group to move up to the executive suites for food, mercifully sparing him from having to answer Kevin.

The tour was one of the scheduled times for parents and guardians to interact with the team. A good time for him to talk with Angela without drawing suspicious looks from Keri, which reminded him of the other reason he shouldn't have kissed Angela. He didn't want to jeopardize Cory's chance to remain in the program any more than she did. He'd had to leave camp early the day after the kiss and hadn't gotten a chance to talk with her the rest of the week. But in the days since he'd known he needed to address what had happened in that locker room. He didn't want to lead her on.

The problem was, he didn't want to let her go, either.

They made it to the executive suite, where business moguls and movie stars typically watched the Gators play. Many of the parents were already there. The kids ran to them, showing pictures on their phones and telling stories about behind the scenes in the auditorium with bright smiles and excited voices.

Isaiah scanned the crowd and found Angela talking to Cory in the middle of the room. Her light laughter at something Cory said brought a smile to his lips. Maroon pants molded to her curvaceous hips and thighs. A short-sleeved black lacy blouse draped over full breasts and provided tempting glimpses of smooth skin. She was so damn sexy.

He should mingle and talk with the other parents. That was the right thing to do as camp host, but he headed straight to her and Cory.

They both glanced his way, their expressions open and welcoming. He met Angela's gaze and felt a hitch in his chest. The subtle shade of red on her lips enhanced their fullness. Brought to mind memories of how great they'd tasted. Desire tightened and flexed like a tiger ready to strike inside him. His pants felt tighter, and he ignored the urge to tuck at his waistband. No need to bring attention to what was happening there.

Cory spoke as soon as Isaiah walked up. "Mr. Isaiah, I was just telling Auntie about the tour. Maybe you could show her around so she could see everything."

Angela shook her head. "That's not necessary. I'm just happy you all got to see it."

"I wouldn't mind showing you around." Why in the world had he offered that?

Because of all the halls and empty rooms you could kiss her in.

"Maybe one day," Angela said. "After camp is over and you have more flexibility."

There was a hopeful note to her voice. The underlying implication clear. Would they finish what they started when Cory's spot was no longer a question? The right answer was no. The answer he wanted to give was hell yes. What would be the harm in keeping his options open with Angela in case things didn't work out with Bridget?

Now you sound like Will. You are not a player.

"Hey, there's Denise." Cory turned to Angela. "I'll be right back." He hurried across the room to talk her.

Angela chuckled. "Is that the girl you told me about?"

Thank goodness for distractions. "Yes. She's the one."

"She's cute. She doesn't seem annoyed that he came over. I hope she likes him, too. I'm not ready for a teenage heartbreak." Angela watched her nephew with interest and a little concern.

"You don't have to worry about that—at least, not yet. I think she likes him."

"I have no idea how much of *the talk* my brother or his mother gave him." A panicked look crossed her face. "Crap, *I* may have to give him *the talk.*"

Isaiah instinctively brushed her arm in comfort. Her skin was soft with the firmness of toned muscle beneath. Her breathing increased. Was that because of his touch or remaining worry for Cory? His hand wanted to linger, caress, and savor the softness of her skin. With effort, he made himself slowly pull back.

"I don't think you need to do that. I've overheard some of the boys talk. He knows the basics."

Angela's chest rose and fell with quick breaths. "Knowing the basics is nothing close to knowing how to not toy with a girl's emotions, or get his toyed with. No one likes to be played for a fool, ya know?"

He did. Which was why he shouldn't have touched or kissed her. Why he had to tell her about Bridget. "I've been wanting to talk—"

"Oh, I want to show you something." She said at the same time. She'd opened her purse to dig something out. She pulled out a sheet of paper that looked like it had been torn out of a magazine.

"What's that?"

"It was in this local magazine we get in the office. They had an article about an underwater filmmaker doing a documentary about sharks off the coast of Florida. He's going to be in our area. I remembered you love sharks and thought you'd find this interesting."

She handed the paper to him. Isaiah scanned the article, then returned his gaze to meet hers. "You remembered that?"

"I thought it was kind of cool that your favorite animal is a shark." She licked full lips and took a deep breath. "Maybe after camp, we can talk about that some more, too."

This was the perfect time to put a halt to things. Tell her about Bridget. Say the kiss was mistake. The words stuck like peanut butter in his throat. He hated peanut butter.

"I'd like that," he replied. The words were wrong. Saying them made him wrong, but damn, if he couldn't stop thinking about her, then maybe he shouldn't stop.

She let out a soft sigh that made him wonder if she'd been holding her breath. Was she nervous? Then she smiled and it was so beautiful and perfect he knew he had to tell her the truth. He never wanted to play with her emotions.

"I need to tell you something," he said.

Arms wrapped around his waist from behind. A female body pressed against his back. "Surprise." Bridget's voice. His body went into panic mode.

Angela's eyes widened. She took a step back. Isaiah felt scorching hot then freezing cold in the span of three seconds. Damn! This was not how things were supposed to go down.

Isaiah unwrapped Bridget's arms and pulled her around to his front. "Bridget, hey, you're here a day early."

Bridget smiled a little too brightly and slipped her arm through his. She was nearly his height in heels, with striking features and a confidence that had only grown over the years he'd known her. Her natural curls were pulled up in a ponytail on top of her head and there wasn't a crease in her cream blouse and gray slacks.

The exuberant welcome was unexpected. All of their conversations had been a little awkward since she'd admitted to being more excited about the job offer than coming here for him. She glanced at Angela and a flash of possessiveness hit her light brown gaze. Exuberance explained. Bridget had always served as his block for unwelcome attention from groupies. He used to appreciate it.

"I was able to snag an earlier flight and decided to surprise you. I like to meet the kids you work with." She glanced back at Angela and held out her free had. "Hello, I'm Bridget. And you are?"

Angela stiffly took Bridget's hand. "Angela. My nephew is part of the program. Are you one of the volunteers?"

Bridget's laugh was so sharp with condescension it could have sliced steel. "No, I'm Isaiah's girlfriend."

Angela's negative head-shake was so slight he would have missed it if he hadn't watched her so hard. An ashen cast dulled her vibrant skin. Guilt and self-loathing created an acidic cocktail in his stomach.

"Oh." Angela took a step back and glanced at Isaiah. "Well, I better go meet this girl that my nephew likes so much."

Questions filled her eyes. He didn't know what to say. There were no words. He had asked Bridget back but they hadn't put a name on what they would be when she returned. Still, he couldn't call Bridget a liar in front of Angela. Hurt flashed over Angela's features before she quickly walked away.

Bridget turned to him. "Looks like I got here just in time."

"Why do you say that?" The words were tight. He focused on Bridget, but the urge to go after Angela and say…something was like an itch he couldn't reach.

"I saw how she looked at you. Another desperate woman trying to latch onto a basketball star. You can thank me later for stepping in. I know you hate women like that." Bridget pulled her arm out of his and glanced around the room. "Introduce me to some of your friends and tell me how camp is going."

Just like that, Bridget had dismissed Angela, viewing her as no sort of threat when really, Angela threatened everything he'd planned for the next step in his life. Before her, a life with Bridget had been his safe, secure and happy future. One conversation, one kiss and a simmering attraction later, and he was ready to throw away years of stability and companionship?

Isaiah looked into Bridget's eyes. He didn't feel the swell of need, excitement or longing he felt with Angela, but he did feel the trust, respect and, yes, happiness he usually felt when they reconnected. Just as anyone would when one of their best friends came to town. They needed to talk about their future—if they had a future—but now wasn't the place.

"Let's start with Coach Gray," Isaiah said and took Bridget over to where Coach was talking with some of the parents.

Chapter 10

I'm Isaiah's girlfriend.

"Nope, not this morning," Angela mumbled to herself and hurried from the car into the office ten minutes late the next morning.

She tugged on the waistband of her skirt and grunted because no amount of tugging would make the skirt any looser. She swore everything in her closet had shrunk overnight. That's what she got for eating half a tub of ice cream and a bag of potato chips before going to bed. Cory decided to move slower than a sloth on sleeping pills this morning, which certainly contributed to her being late and exhausted, though really it was that she'd been tossing and turning all night.

Learning the vibe she'd felt between her and Isaiah was all in her imagination hadn't set her up for a good night's sleep. He'd only been messing with her while he dated some tall, beautiful, I'm-so-polished-you-might-as-well-call-me-spit-shine woman. She was such an idiot for kissing him.

She rushed through the front door and speed-walked down to her office. No one stopped her to say good morning. *Good.* She wasn't in the mood to talk. She put her stuff up and turned on her computer to go through emails.

The office was quiet. Unusual for first thing in the morning. There was always at least ten to fifteen minutes of people chitchatting before they got to work. She checked her calendar. Nothing scheduled.

Footsteps sounded outside her door before her supervisor, Tamara, poked her head in. "Angela, what are you doing in here?"

Tamara's light brown eyes widened and she came farther into Angela's office. Four-inch heels added additional height to her small curvy frame. She had a fondness for animal print, often throwing in a zebra- or leopard-print scarf or shoes, like the ones she wore today with tan slacks and a black button-up.

"I was running a little late."

Tamara waved her hand, indicating Angela needed to move. "Come on. Mr. Cooper called a meeting. The director from the Columbia office is here to talk about our cross-training with his team. We're gathering in the conference room."

Angela cringed but jumped from the chair. "I thought they weren't coming until next week." She grabbed her notebook and a pen before popping up from her desk.

"So did I, but you know how Mr. Cooper likes to spring things on us."

Angela followed her supervisor down the hall to the conference room. A man she didn't recognize paused in the middle of speaking and watched as she and Tamara entered. He was tall, midthirties with mahogany skin, and was dressed business-casual in a green polo and dark gray slacks. He paused long enough to bring attention to their late entrance before he continued talking.

Mr. Cooper's angry green gaze could have boiled water in Antarctica. The perfect embodiment of a pious and judgmental person, Mr. Cooper only lost his pinched expression when he was helping kids. For him, relaxed was a cartoon tie instead of a standard blue or red one with his dark brown suits. But he cared about their office and the kids, so Angela excused his uptightness.

There was no seating left, so Angela stood in a corner. She listened as the speaker, Alvin, talked about how his office had increased volunteer participation. The work they'd done was impressive, and Angela's frazzled feelings from coming to work late slowly faded as excitement grew with the idea of helping to take their office to the same level.

Mr. Cooper stood after Alvin finished his talk. "Thank you, Alvin. You all know why we invited his crew down—to do more with our volunteers and help more kids. So we're going to require commitment from everyone on the team on this. Starting today." He stared pointedly at Angela.

Embarrassment burned her cheeks, but she returned his stare with an optimistic one. She was late today, but she would make this work. She wanted to continue working here, hopefully as a case manager once she completed her graduate degree. Coming in late today was not the best start to this project, but she didn't want Mr. Cooper to doubt her commitment.

"Alvin and his team will meet with each of you individually to go over your volunteer files and get an idea of ways to improve their participation. Because we can't afford to shut the office down for a day, we'll have meetings after business hours to compare notes and run training. The first meeting is today at six, so Alvin can go into more detail regarding which of his team members will work with each of you and strategize for the best use of their time while they're here."

Six! Angela pulled out her cell phone and navigated

to her calendar even though she already knew what her schedule looked like. She was off at Sweethearts, which meant she hadn't asked Nate to watch Cory for her. She quickly texted him to see if he could, and he answered right back.

Sorry, Angela, but I've got a meeting tonight.

Crap, what was she going to do about Cory?

"Ms. Bouler, is there a problem?" Mr. Cooper's voice cut into her thoughts.

Angela slipped her cell into her pocket. "No, sir."

"Good."

He spoke for another few minutes. Angela went over every possible scenario she could think of as to what to do with Cory. She could call Vicki, but she probably had to work tonight. There were evening child-watch programs, but if Cory thought he was too big for a babysitter, he'd definitely balk at the idea of her leaving him at an evening day care.

The meeting finally ended and Angela hurried out of the conference room instead of staying behind to talk more with the group about logistics.

Mr. Cooper followed her out. "Angela, a second."

She skidded to a halt, took a deep breath, then turned and faced him. "Yes, sir."

Mr. Cooper's expression was still pinched and disapproving. If Angela hadn't known him to light up with joy whenever they helped a kid, she'd wonder why he even worked in their office. "You seemed distracted in there," he said. "Are you going to have a problem with helping to improve this office?"

"Not at all."

"Then why were you staring at your phone?"

"I'm not sure if you're aware, but I've recently had to take temporary custody of my nephew. He's thirteen and I don't have anyone to watch him tonight. I texted a friend to see if they could help out."

Mr. Cooper's eyebrows drew together. "I understand that, but I need your full commitment on this project. If you want to be a case manager one day, then you need to make sure your personal life doesn't interfere with your work here."

Angela gritted her teeth. Her commitment had never been a question before. She had the best volunteer participation rate and it wasn't as if everyone didn't know she was the one to step in with other people's volunteers when they were having trouble.

"I've always been committed to what we do. I know what these kids are facing and that's why I want to be an advocate for them."

"Then you above anyone understands why I don't like for my employees to bring their own family problems to work?" The cool reprimand cut her to the quick. Mr. Cooper was unmarried with no kids of his own so he wasn't very flexible when it came to family emergencies from his employees. Their advocacy work was his entire life, and maybe unfairly, he expected it to be the same for his employees. She didn't usually deal with him directly and thankfully Tamara was more understanding.

Don't take it personally. He's like this with everyone. That knowledge didn't make her feel any less guilty for coming in late. "I'll work everything out with Cory."

"Good. I'll see you at the six-o'clock meeting. On time." He turned and walked away.

Angela balled her hands into fists and bared her teeth to the back of his head. Taking a deep breath, she turned away and walked back to her office. It was still early. She had time to find someone who could watch Cory while she worked late. At least this would keep her mind off of Isaiah.

Yeah, right, you're thinking about him right now.

Angela huffed out a breath, pushed Isaiah from her thoughts and focused on the myriad of challenges ahead.

For the first time in the years he'd volunteered for the Gators' basketball camp, Isaiah was glad to see the day end. He rubbed his tired eyes and yawned while he walked to the storage area in the back of the center to put up the balls. He didn't have to help with the cleanup at the end of the day, but he always wanted to show his thanks to the camp counselors, who put up with the hassle of securing the facility and keeping the public, who continued to use the facility while the Gators held camp, separate from the players and the kids in the camp.

Today he wished he could be a little selfish and rush out like most of the other players. But just because he hadn't slept well and struggled to not snap at people like an angry alligator didn't mean he had to skip out on helping.

Keri walked out of the storage room just as he was getting ready to go in. "I can take those from you." She reached for the bag of basketballs in Isaiah's hand.

"I'm already back here. I can put them up."

She stepped aside and let Isaiah open the door. "How are you doing today?" The question was simple but her tone was wary.

Isaiah put the balls on the right shelf and leaned against the door of the room. "I'm fine. Why do you ask like that?"

"You seemed a little…off today."

He ran a hand over his face. "Sorry, I didn't sleep well last night. I'm a little tired today."

"I hope there isn't anything about the camp that's wearing you down. The kids, our schedule, one of the parents or guardians…" Her eyebrows rose and she tilted her head to the side when she said *guardians*.

No question which guardian she was referring to. He'd tossed and turned last night thinking about the hurt expression in Angela's eyes after Bridget said they were dating. Why the hell did he feel bad about that? He'd planned on telling her. He should have been glad to get the entire thing over with. Except, after the function Bridget had said she was tired and went back to her hotel room. They'd exchanged an awkward hug and quick kiss before parting and hadn't talked since. Or, maybe the hug and kiss were awkward because he'd felt guilty for hurting Angela. The woman he shouldn't be thinking about.

He gave Keri a reassuring smile and closed the door to the storage room. "Nothing like that. Everything is going great at camp. Just up late watching some movie on television. I'll be going to bed early tonight."

Keri seemed satisfied with that explanation. They chatted about plans for the next day as they walked to the front of the activity center. Isaiah stopped and signed a few autographs for some people at the front desk, Keri's ultimate destination, before he waved goodbye and left the center.

Outside, the heat and humidity cloaked him instantly in sweat. He and Bridget hadn't made any plans for tonight, but they needed to talk. He needed to figure out what his next move would be. After a shower and something to eat, he'd call her and see if she wanted to meet for dinner.

He headed to his car, but was surprised to find Cory

and Denise standing at the edge of the sidewalk. Denise's older sister had signed her out of camp earlier. Cory should have been inside waiting on his aunt.

Cory held his cell phone to his ear. Denise leaned in and watched Cory with an eager expression.

"Come on, Auntie, I'm almost fourteen. I can stay home by myself," Cory said into the phone.

Isaiah slowed his steps and listened, unashamedly, to Cory's side of the phone call.

"Do you know how many thirteen-year-olds stay home alone? Everyone in my class does. Besides you said you'll only be working 'til seven or seven thirty. I can handle that amount of time alone." Cory got quiet and listened. He smiled and took Denise's hand in his. "Don't worry. I'll just be watching television and playing video games." Cory winked at Denise, who bounced on the tips of her toes.

Playing video games and watching TV, his ass. Cory was trying to sneak Denise to his home. Isaiah shook his head and walked over to them both. "Tell your aunt not to worry. I'll watch you until she gets off work."

Startled, Cory jumped and quickly dropped Denise's hand. "Oh, hey, Mr. Isaiah."

"Did you hear what I said? I can watch you until your aunt is off work," Isaiah repeated.

Cory's eyes widened with excitement. He shot a quick glance at Denise. Isaiah could read the conflict on his face. "Really? You'll let me hang with you?"

"I'll look forward to it. I'd rather you hang out with me than have your aunt worry about you being home alone. We'll do exactly what you said, watch television and play video games."

"Cool! Auntie, Mr. Isaiah says I can hang with him." The excitement in Cory's voice was obvious. The grimace on Denise's face, followed by her sucking her teeth, also obviously displayed her annoyance. Isaiah felt no guilt for interrupting their teenage dream.

Thank goodness Cory was still young enough to put hanging out and playing video games above alone time with his girlfriend. In a few years, that may not be the case.

Cory listened to his aunt on the phone. His exuberant smile dwindled to a disappointed frown. "I didn't ask him. He offered…Why not? You were just worried about me being home alone…Come on! Don't be like that."

Isaiah held out his hand. "Give me the phone. Let me talk to her." Cory handed over the phone. "Angela, hey, it's Isaiah."

He heard her quick inhalation. Had anger or something else made her do that? "I'm sorry if Cory asked you to hang out. Believe me I will tell him not to impose on you anymore. I'll figure out someplace for him to go tonight." Her tone was brisk. The lack of warmth made him want to squirm. He'd hurt her.

"It wasn't Cory who asked. I overheard him talking to you, and I think it's best if he spent time with me instead of being home alone."

"Why, what's wrong?" Her voice sharpened with worry.

Isaiah glanced at Cory and Denise; Cory excited, Denise glaring daggers at Cory. "Denise's sister signed her out already. I'll make sure she's still here before Cory and I leave," he said slowly, hoping she picked up on what he inferred. "That way Cory won't have to wait with her alone."

"Crap, was he planning to bring her back to my place?"

He was glad she'd caught on quickly. "I'm not sure,

but I know he'll have a good time with me and I'll keep him out of trouble."

Angela sighed. "What about your girlfriend? Will she have a problem with you spending time with Cory after camp?"

"Bridget and I haven't officially been together for over a year. She just moved to the area yesterday. I'm still very free to hang with whomever I want on my own time."

"Oh, really?" She sounded skeptical.

"Really. I'll have Cory text you my address. Come over when you're off work."

"You're taking him to your place?"

"Yes, it's more secure than your place. I don't want to cause a scene."

"That's right. I forgot you're a famous basketball star."

"Believe me, the famous part is more inconvenience than anything. I don't want to make things difficult for you and Cory. Are you cool with him coming with me?"

She hesitated. He wished he could scc hcr face. To see if she was worried about imposing on his time, or because she didn't want to have to see him.

"I'm cool with that."

He had to fight not to let out a heavy sigh. He hadn't completely ruined her trust in him. "Great. We'll see you when you get off."

He liked the idea of being there to help her out. To provide a shoulder for her to lean on in a time of need. He liked that feeling a lot, but hadn't that always been a problem for him? Jumping in to save the day without regard to consequences?

"Isaiah…thank you."

The relief in her voice made him feel like he was a superhero who'd just saved her from harm. He pictured her angelic smile and bright eyes. Consequences be damned. "You're welcome, Angel." He used her nickname on purpose. "I'll see you when you get off work."

Chapter 11

"Let's be real, you were trying to sneak Denise over to your aunt's place tonight," Isaiah said to Cory.

They stood in Isaiah's upstairs media room, each holding electronic guns pointed at the television, where a virtual military unit carried out a rescue mission. They'd been playing the video game for the past half hour.

Cory glanced quickly at Isaiah before shooting a few villains in the game. "She mentioned coming over just to hang out."

Isaiah smirked. "Uh-huh, just hang out. How did you get out of camp without your aunt signing you out?"

Cory looked sheepish. "Denise's sister."

"Not cool, Cory. If you get caught sneaking out, Keri may put you and Denise out of the program and get your aunt in a lot of trouble. Do you want that?" Isaiah made a mental note to tell Keri what happened anyway so she could handle it with the young people signing kids in and out at the end of the day.

Cory dropped his hands and turned to Isaiah with wide, worried eyes. "I'm sorry. I didn't think about that. It's just… Denise really wanted to hang out with me."

Cory's character on screen was taken out while he processed Isaiah's warning. Teenage hormones were a dangerous thing and could lead to bad decisions. Hopefully the threat of getting him or his aunt in trouble would curb future attempts to sneak out of camp.

"What were you going to do once you got Denise back to your place?" Isaiah focused back on not being the next causality on the game.

Cory shrugged in Isaiah's periphery. "I don't know. Just talk and chill." Cory went back to playing the game.

"Talk and chill, sure. Look, man, don't bring girls to your aunt's place. Especially when she's not home and doesn't know someone is coming over. You don't want her to have a reason not to trust you, do you?"

"No," Cory said sullenly. "I got excited when Denise wanted to come over. I've never had a girl ask to come over before."

"I understand, but are you really ready to be *alone* with a girl?" No sense in pretending he didn't know what Cory was really interested in doing with a girl over.

"I don't know. All the guys I know say I'd be crazy to not want to, you know…be alone with her. I don't want to seem like I'm scared. Because I'm not," Cory said in a rush.

Isaiah understood the false bravado. He'd been excited and scared about the idea of being alone with a girl, much less doing stuff with her. Thankfully, he'd had his dad and brother to talk to. Cory didn't have either.

"It's not about being scared, but it's okay to be unsure about rushing into anything. You should always talk things out with someone you trust if you're feeling pressured into anything"

"Who can I talk to? My dad is in jail. My mom skipped out on me. And I can't bring any of this up with Auntie without it being weird." Defeat filled Cory's voice. He fired several virtual rounds and wiped out the remaining villains in the game. His shoulders sagged and he lowered the controller.

Isaiah put his own virtual gun on the mahogany coffee table and placed a hand on Cory's shoulder. "Hey, you can always talk to me."

Cory used his eye roll to say whatever. "Camp only lasts a few more weeks. After that, you're back to being a famous basketball star. It's been really cool hanging out here, but I know you won't have time."

He tried to pull away and Isaiah held on to the boy's shoulder. "I don't make promises I won't keep. I'll give you my number. If you ever need a man to talk to, don't hesitate to reach out to me. You've got a lot of promise, Cory. Don't let your current circumstances bring you down. You hear me?"

Cory's nod was hesitant, but a hopeful light came to his eyes. "You're really going to give me your number?"

Isaiah tilted his head to the side. "I'm going to trust you with it. You aren't going to pass it out to every kid you know or show it to girls like Denise to impress them?"

Cory stood straight and met Isaiah's eye. "No, sir. I wouldn't do you like that. Not after you've been so helpful to me."

The doorbell rang. "Good. That must be the food." He dropped his hand from Cory's shoulder. "Play another game while I grab it, okay."

"Can I wear your headset?" Cory pointed to a headset that would let him hear and communicate with online players.

"Sure, you're better than me at this game anyway. Go ahead and hook up with an online team."

Isaiah left Cory in the media room and ran downstairs to meet the pizza-delivery person. He didn't regret his promise. His mom used to chastise him for playing the hero. Cory's situation wasn't his business, but he liked the teen. Saw in him the same awkward kid he'd once been, but where Isaiah had the support of his family, Cory just had Angela, who was more than capable, but he didn't want Cory to feel as if he didn't have a man he could reach out to.

He paid the delivery guy, then took the pizza, wings, bread sticks and sodas upstairs to the game room. Cory continued to battle bad guys in a virtual jungle, so Isaiah went back downstairs to grab plates, napkins and cups.

He had all the stuff in hand with one foot on the bottom stair when the doorbell rang again. Isaiah went to the door and checked the peephole. His heart dribbled in his chest. Angela.

He shifted the items in his hands and unlocked the door before opening it wide. Her hair hung loose around her shoulders, and she wore a navy pencil skirt with a light blue short-sleeved blouse tucked into the waistband. The outfit emphasized her small waist, round hips and full breasts. Heels gave her height and turned her legs into weapons of male destruction.

His body melted like hot candle wax. The urge to pull her close and kiss those full lips ran over him like a defensive player.

"Hey, is Cory ready?" Her voice and expression were neutral.

He missed the warmth she'd shown before and her welcoming smile. "He's upstairs playing a game. Our dinner just got here." He nodded for her to come in and stepped back. "Come on up."

"I really don't want to intrude."

"You're not intruding. There's plenty of food to go around. No need to waste it."

She hesitated before stepping just inside the door. Her soft, sexy perfume tickled his senses, begged him to kiss along her neck and drown in the sweet scent. She glanced left and right, her eyes wary. "We can take some to go."

"This isn't a drive-through," he teased. "You've worked a long day. Sit down and relax for a little."

The argument formed in her eyes. He stepped forward and pushed the door closed with his foot. The movement brought him closer. They almost touched, which made him more aware of her than actually touching. He breathed in the scent of her perfume and fought not to lean farther into her space.

He stepped back, otherwise he might give in to the impulse. "Will you lock that for me?"

He turned and walked toward the stairs before she could give another reason for why she couldn't stay. A few tense seconds passed, then the lock clicked. Isaiah released a breath. He glanced at her over his shoulder and waited for her to join him at the stairs.

"Is anyone else here?" she asked.

He shook his head. "Just me and Cory." He met her gaze. "No one stays here but me."

She glanced away quickly, but he saw the small lift of her full lips. His friends would say he didn't owe her an explanation, but he wanted her to know Bridget didn't live with him.

When they entered the game room, Cory was completely engrossed in the game. Angela walked over to him and waved her hand to get his attention. He smiled at her and fired a couple of shots at the screen.

"Are we leaving?" He still had the headset on so his voice was raised.

Angela pointed to her watch. "We've got to get back home."

Cory slid the headset off one ear. "Just a few more minutes. I'm almost done with this mission. Please."

Angela huffed and raised her hands in a conciliatory gesture. "Fine. Five minutes."

Cory grinned, nodded and slid the headset back before returning to the game. Isaiah set the paper plates and utensils on the table. He motioned for Angela to take a seat with him. She sat on the edge of the sofa, her arms and shoulders stiff.

"I want to talk to you about yesterday," Isaiah said. Moreover, he *needed* to talk to her about yesterday. He wasn't a player. He didn't want her to think he was.

Angela glanced at Cory. "You don't owe me an explanation."

"Cory can't hear us. He's all into that game." Isaiah pulled one leg onto the couch and faced Angela. "And I do owe you an explanation."

She tucked her hair behind her ear. "Look, I thought about everything and you really don't owe me anything. I kissed you and I shouldn't have. I didn't know you were in a relationship."

"I kissed you back."

Her spine stiffened and her eyes hardened. "I don't play the other woman."

"I'm not asking you to be my other woman. I'm not a player. I leave that for the other guys on the team."

"Then why did you kiss me back?"

"Because I like you," he said honestly. "But, I've known Bridget since college. We dated then, and off and on after I was drafted. A little over a year ago, we took a break while she finished law school, but we still kept in touch."

Angela smirked and flipped her hair. "Kept in touch? We're adults—you two continued to hook up."

He shook his head. "It wasn't like that. I dated other women and I haven't seen Bridget in months. I prefer to keep things simple without any drama. My relationship with Bridget has always been simple." He waited for a response, but Angela didn't say anything. "Before her graduation, I asked her to consider moving to Jacksonville so we could try having a relationship again. She agreed, got a job here and moved back this week."

"Are you in love with her?" Angela asked.

Isaiah considered the words, but he already knew the answer. They'd been apart for a while. He had love for Bridget, and he'd figured her coming to town would give them both the chance to fall in love with each other again. "I care about her."

Angela's stare was skeptical. "But you asked her to move here. That must mean you feel a little more for her than care."

"I trust Bridget. A guy in my position can't be too careful when it comes to relationships. People are always trying to get a piece of you. I didn't want to go through the trouble of figuring out if a woman was into me or what I can do for her. I don't have to worry about that with Bridget."

"What about love, passion, fire?" She toyed absently with the circular charm of her necklace. The movement drew his eye to her cleavage. He might have thought she was teasing him on purpose, except for the genuine confusion in her voice.

Isaiah forced his attention from the lush brown skin of her décolletage back to her face. "Just as important as mutual respect, stability and comfort."

Angela brought the charm to her nose for a few seconds, then dropped it and shook her head. "If I ever get married, I plan to have all of that. I won't settle for just being with a guy because it's comfortable."

As much as he didn't want to think about her married to another man, her statement piqued his curiosity. "If? You don't think you'll get married one day?"

"I'm not sure I want to get married." She reached over to the pizza box and lifted the top. "I'm not into the idea of being dependent on someone. I like being able to take care of myself and doing what I want without answering to anyone else."

"That's not what marriage is about," he said, slightly amused by her defiant tone. "Marriage is a mutual partnership."

She gave him a *whatever* smirk. "Someone is always expected to give more in any partnership. You know I'm telling the truth because you're smiling."

"I'm smiling because I hope you're joking. What you're describing is called compromise. When you love someone you're willing to give on things."

She chuckled. "Okay, what would you be willing to compromise?" She put a slice of pizza on a paper plate and handed it to him.

Isaiah took the plate. He met her beautiful eyes, sparkling with amusement, and answered without thought. "Anything to make you happy."

Her eyes widened. Then her amusement swirled to what he thought was longing before her brows drew together and she looked away. Embarrassment flooded his system.

"You know what I mean," he said quickly. "I'd do whatever was necessary to make whomever I'm with happy."

Angela put another slice of pizza on a plate. "I think staying away from me would make Bridget happy."

"But it won't make me happy." Apparently, he was just going to say whatever came to his mind right now.

Angela put the plate in her lap. They were quiet while she pulled the pepperoni off the pizza. "Me, neither, but you asked her here," she said in a resigned tone. "I can tell you're not the type of guy to mess with me while you're still involved with her." She met his gaze. "And I'm not the type of woman who'll come between you two."

She was right. Everything good, and noble, and gentlemanly in him said to agree. But he didn't want to be gentlemanly. He wanted to keep Angela in his life. Wanted Angela to be the woman in his life.

A rush of adrenaline hit him harder than his first professional game. A mixture of fear, excitement and panic sent his pulse into overdrive. Was he ready to give up the history he had with Bridget for this intense, fiery feeling he had for Angela? Was he making a mistake to consider this, or would walking away be the bigger mistake? He needed time to think, time to consider, before he did something he'd regret forever.

"I called the producer in that documentary," he said with a casualness he didn't feel.

Her shoulders relaxed. He couldn't tell if she was disappointed because she focused on the pizza again. "Really? How did it go?"

"He may let me come out on the boat with them when they search for sharks off the coast."

"That sounds really scary, but also kind of cool. Why do you love sharks so much?" She took a small bite of the pizza.

Isaiah leaned back into the couch, comfortable with a nonlife-changing topic. "Because they're big, strong and graceful. When a great white comes into the area, all other animals hide. They aren't afraid of anything because there aren't many things that can hurt them. They're the ultimate embodiment of confidence."

She swallowed, nodded and licked pizza sauce off her lips. "I guess I can see that."

His gaze had followed the movement of her tongue and his cock twitched with interest. He shifted in his seat. "I'd love to work with him on this. Maybe even get a spot on the documentary he's doing. It's supposed to air during Shark Week."

Angela's eyes widened. She'd just taken another bite and placed her hand in front of her mouth. "I may see you on Shark Week?"

Her enthusiasm brought a grin to his lips. "You watch Shark Week?"

"Every year since I was eleven. It'd be so cool to actually know someone on one of the shows."

"I've watched it every year, too—obviously. My family thinks I'm crazy for being into sharks. They would really lose their minds if they knew I'd love to get into underwater filmmaking after I retire."

"Why? That would be the coolest job," she said as if underwater filmmaking was all the rage.

"My parents are college professors. Engineering and mathematics, which means they're both very practical. They think my journalism degree would better serve me in broadcast journalism when I retire. I agree, but after a career playing ball, which I love, I'd like to retire into another career I'd love. Broadcasting isn't something I'm interested in."

And speaking of his parents, they'd think he was being impractical for even considering breaking things off permanently with Bridget in order to be with Angela. Regardless of her job advocating for kids, all his parents would see was her work at a strip club. They'd warned him off groupies and gold diggers from the second it became obvious he was gifted with a basketball. If they found out he'd met Angela there, they wouldn't care about his feelings and would assume he was making a decision with the head between his legs.

"Forget what they want, go for what you want," Angela said. "You've only got one life—don't spend it making other people happy. In the end, they won't be the one living with the regret. I'd rather do things on my terms. That way if things go bad then I'm the only one to blame. Don't give others control. Believe that you're strong enough to survive any mistakes."

"Is that how you live your life?"

She looked down at her wrist, at the symbol of strength. "If you're afraid every decision you make may be the wrong one, then you won't make any decisions. After having someone make a decision that nearly ruined my future and then bouncing back from that, I trust myself and any choices I make for myself a little more."

What regrets would he be left with? Ever since his hero antics, as his dad called them, when he was younger, he hadn't made a move without thinking of the consequences. All because he was worried of how the consequences would affect other people. His parents, his teammates, his relationships. Would his actions upset his parents, upset his coaches and upset his career. When was the last time he'd gone for what he wanted, consequences be damned? Angela leaned forward to grab a can of soda. Were the consequences of telling Bridget that asking her to move here was a mistake enough to stop him from doing it? From getting closer to Angela?

Cory yelled and jumped up and down. He yanked off the headset and spun around to face them. "We took out the entire unit! This game is so cool."

Angela laughed and put her plate on the coffee table. "Well, if you've taken out the unit, then you've finished the level, and we can go."

Cory pointed to the pizza. "I didn't eat."

"We can take it with us." She glanced at her watch. "It's getting late and we've imposed on Isaiah long enough." She stood.

Isaiah stood, as well. He wasn't ready for her to leave. "You don't have to go."

She shook her head, but her smile was regretful. "I'm tired and I really want to get home and get out of these heels. Come on, Cory. Grab a few slices and we'll go."

Isaiah didn't argue. He needed time to think, consider. If he was about to say consequences be damned, he needed a clear head. He gave Angela the second pizza and told her to take it since he wasn't going to eat both of them, then walked them to the door.

Angela stopped at the door and gave him an unguarded smile that brightened his world. "Thanks again, Isaiah."

"It was no problem at all." He wanted to hug her goodbye. Wanted the privilege of being able to kiss her goodbye. He wanted her and he couldn't keep ignoring that. "Drive safe, okay?"

After Angela and Cory left he called Bridget. She answered on the third ring. "Hey, Isaiah, what's up?" Bridget said in a cheery voice, though the "what's up?" came in a tone that made him feel like he needed to get to a point.

"I thought we could get together."

"Oh." Was that hesitation in her tone? "It was just that I'm about to head out. I'm meeting a few of my new co-workers for drinks."

"You haven't even started yet and you're meeting co-workers for drinks?" He couldn't hide his surprise. She didn't start her job until the following week and she'd already met her coworkers?

She gave a little laugh. "One of my undergraduate friends works at Goldman Schultz. She's actually the one who put me on the job. I'm meeting up with her to get the skinny before I start."

He hadn't known that, but honestly, he hadn't asked her much about the job. He hadn't given much thought to Bridget's life in Jacksonville outside of their relationship. The realization didn't make him feel very good. Had he only been treating Bridget like a check-off on his things to do before the season started? "Why don't you come over? Let's talk."

"About what?"

"Us."

"Oh." Again the hesitation, and a hint of concern. "You know, Isaiah, we do need to talk, but not tonight."

He ignored the relief he felt that she didn't want to come over. That couldn't be a good sign. He shouldn't have asked her to move here. Which meant he wasn't looking forward to her reaction when he told her so.

"You know what? That's no problem," he said. "I had a long day at the camp. Let's get together tomorrow."

"Sure, yes, tomorrow's great." Relief in her voice, too. "Good night, Isaiah."

"Good night, Bridget."

Chapter 12

Isaiah didn't run into Angela the next day. One second Cory was there and the next he was gone. Checked out by his aunt, he confirmed with Keri. Angela must be avoiding him. Not what he wanted, but he understood. To her, he was unavailable. Not for long. Regardless of the consequences he was talking to Bridget tonight.

He showered at the center, then went directly to the condo Bridget had rented. He knocked and after a few minutes, Bridget answered with a hesitant smile. She had on a pair of tiny pink shorts and a gray tank top with the words *I don't sweat, I glisten* on the front.

Bridget stepped aside and let him in. He leaned in to hug her, but she was already turning away. "Oh…sorry," she said and turned back.

They both leaned in with their torsos. Bridget patted him on the back twice. A church hug, according to Will. The kind of hug a woman gave you when she didn't want to get too close. Maybe that was a good sign.

They broke apart and Bridget stepped back. "I'm still unpacking." She pointed to the boxes stacked in the room. "Can I get you anything?"

"No, I'm good." He followed her farther into the condo.

"Okay." She stopped in front of the white linen sofa in the living room. "Have a seat."

Isaiah did and ran his hands over his khaki shorts. His shirt was a lightweight white T-shirt but sweat ran down his back. "So…getting settled in?"

"Mmm-hmm." She nodded. "I really like the condo. I don't think I'll look for a more permanent place anytime soon."

"That's good. I'm glad you like it here." Maybe she wouldn't be too angry when he told her that they shouldn't get back together. "Look, Bridget, there's something I want to say."

"Shh…" She straddled his lap and pushed his shoulders back before he could say more. "Let's talk later."

Her lips covered his. He immediately wanted to push her back, but he hesitated. Maybe this was the final test he needed. If he still wanted her, he should feel something when they kissed. So he let her lead. When her tongue tested his lips for a deeper kiss, he opened, then waited for his reaction. When he'd kissed Angela, he'd forgotten everything around them. He'd had a hard time not pulling her harder against him. Angela's kiss had made him crave her. Bridget's kiss was familiar, but not nearly as exciting. Bridget's kiss felt…wrong. The wrong fit for him. Guilt made his body cold.

He opened his eyes and met Bridget's gaze. They broke apart quickly. She lifted her hand to her lips, then dropped it quickly. He understood the reflex. He wanted to wipe away the kiss, too.

"Does this feel…?" He tried to think of something to say.

"Awkward?" Bridget said, finishing his thought. She slid off his lap and scooted to the other side of the couch.

Another word would have been less harsh but he

couldn't think of anything better. "It's been a while since we've been together." The excuse sounded lame.

Bridget sighed and tugged on one of the corkscrew curls in her hair. "It has, but...we've never had chemistry problems before."

"Before, we got together because it was convenient and short-term. This time it's—"

"I don't want to get married." Bridget's brown eyes widened and she slapped a hand over her mouth.

Isaiah wanted to shout his relief. Probably not the best reaction. He nodded slowly. "I don't, either."

Bridget's shoulders relaxed. "I thought you'd freak out."

He turned to face her fully. "No. We've both changed since we last saw each other. Of course what we want has changed, too."

"So you're okay with us just dating instead of jumping straight to something more serious?" Her voice was hopeful.

Isaiah rubbed his chin. "Actually, I need to tell you something."

Her eyebrows shot up. When she rubbed her shoulder, a nervous gesture of hers, the strap of her tank top slid off. "Why do you sound ominous?"

He took a deep breath and said what he needed to say. "There is someone else."

Bridget had been reaching for him. She dropped her hand and jumped from the couch. Her hands slammed onto her hips and her glare sliced him to pieces. "Someone else?" she said, her tone low and angry. "You're seeing someone else?"

Isaiah shifted forward on the couch. "You just said you didn't want to get married."

She nodded, but the anger in her eyes didn't lessen.

"Yeah, because it had been months since we saw each other and when you asked me to come here, you mentioned eventually getting married. Not because I'm seeing someone else. Why did you ask me to move here if you were seeing another woman?"

"I wasn't seeing her when I asked you to move. We met after." He kept his voice neutral. Bridget wasn't one to go off and create a scene when she was angry, but he didn't want to tempt her.

Her eyes narrowed. "Who is she?"

He had no reason to lie. "Her name is Angela."

Bridget took a step back and placed a hand on her chest. "The woman at the center?" She sneered. "I thought she was another groupie trying to get with you."

"She isn't." He fought to keep his calm after the disdain in Bridget's voice. "We click. There's something there. I don't want to ignore it—I don't think I can."

Bridget rolled her eyes and scoffed. "Really, Isaiah? I thought you were smarter than that." She turned away.

Isaiah stood. "What's that supposed to mean?"

She looked at him as if he was crazy. "You've spent years saying you can't deal with these thirsty women who chase you and your teammates, and now one comes around with a pretty face, and an at-risk kid, and you're ready to save a ho."

"She's not a whore." His voice hardened with his anger. "And she doesn't need saving. It's different when I'm with her."

Bridget flipped her wrist dismissively. "You know what? Go get her. See if I give a damn. I knew years ago I was wasting my time with you."

He wasn't sure if the statement was meant to harm or was just her way to deflect her own pain, but either way, it bothered him. "Then why did you come?"

She crossed her arms and tossed up her chin. "I didn't say no because like an idiot I had a soft spot for you. I knew I was your backup. That you were keeping me in your back pocket until you decided you were ready to get married."

"That's not how I treated you. That's not how I thought of you."

"You can lie to me, but don't lie to yourself. I was your safety net. Not because you love me, but because you love the idea of me."

Isaiah clenched his jaw to keep from cursing. He took a deep breath and asked, "What are you talking about?"

"You want what your parents have. Do you think I didn't realize you called and asked me to move here right after your brother got engaged? You've played professional ball, traveled and had your fun. Now you're ready for a wife and kids. What do you do? Call me to come fill the bill." Her voice was cold and sliced him to the quick.

He took a few steps back. "You didn't really want to come."

She lifted her shoulder. "Honestly, the job offer made up my mind."

The admission wasn't a surprise. He'd already wondered if that was the real reason. Maybe even the only reason. "That's it, huh?"

"I did wonder if proximity would have brought us closer. I did love you once." Her voice softened from glacial to freezing rain.

He had loved her once, too. Years ago when they were in college and she was the first woman he'd felt comfortable with. That's why he'd held on to this for so long. The memory of love just as powerful as the actual feelings. Especially for him when the actual feelings made him feel off and unsure. "When did you stop?"

"When I realized our relationship had morphed to just a physical one."

"Did you want more from me?" Something in her voice made him suspect she was only pretending to sound nonchalant. He didn't want to know if he'd hurt her.

"Before we became just occasional hookups, yes, I wanted what you did. But when I started law school, I knew our goals had changed. You still want a perfect wife. Someone who needs you."

His head jerked. That wasn't what he was like. "I don't want that."

"Yes you do, even if you don't see it. You're old-fashioned that way. Just like your dad. You want to take care of things, solve everyone's problems. You'll want a woman who'll rely on you. I'm not that woman. I never will be."

"I never asked you to rely on me."

"But you always swept in to take care of my problems. Maybe that's the other reason I stuck around."

"You used me."

She rolled her eyes. "I'd hardly call it being used when you were so quick to step in before I could even fix the problem. Remember when my car broke down? I just mentioned it in passing and the next day, there was a mechanic at my door. That's just you, Isaiah. I'll admit it's sweet, but it's also proof that you're a fixer. I think it would have eventually broken us... If this woman hadn't broken us first."

"She didn't break us. Apparently we were already broken." He ran a hand over his face. His mind whirled with all the things she'd thrown at him. Regret over hurting her came to the forefront. "Bridget, I'm sorry if I ever hurt you. That wasn't my intention. I really thought we'd make things work one day."

"I know you mean that. Honestly, a part of me wonders if this is just another phase we're going through. Go on, have your fun with her. Let me get settled in and then maybe we can try again."

"That's not what I'm going to do," he said in an exasperated tone. "I'm not playing with her."

Her smile was sweet and sarcastic. "You really believe that, don't you? I'll be curious to see how long that lasts." She cocked her head to the side and considered him. After a second, she nodded. "I've waited this long, and I do need to get settled in. I'll give you six months to get her out of your system. I won't promise to wait around for you, but I'm willing to consider a retry after six months."

She was really dismissing what he had to say.

"Don't wait. We're through." He meant it. No matter what happened with Angela, he knew he couldn't be with Bridget. He'd felt the fire and spark he should feel with a woman; he'd never be able to go back to the safe and convenient relationship he'd had with Bridget. He wanted more from life than bland and boring.

She clasped her hands in front of her chest. "That's cute." She walked past him toward the door. "I'll see you later, Isaiah."

Isaiah left without another word. A part of him hated the way things had ended. He'd never meant to hurt her. He doubted Bridget was in love with him, but her reaction today said she still cared deeply. For that, he would always be sorry. He didn't regret making the break. Another revelation from their conversation was that keeping this going was unfair to both of them. He was ready to do what felt right, not what was expected. Despite Bridget's low expectations, expectations he was sure his family would agree with once they found out, being with Angela felt right. He took a deep, freeing breath. Consequences be damned.

Chapter 13

Angela put another half-dozen drinks on the bar for Star, one of the waitresses at Sweethearts. Star squeezed through the crowd at the club, elbowing a few people out of the way to retrieve them.

Someone pushed her back and Star rolled her eyes. "Tonight is crazy. Thanks so much for having these ready, Angel. The guys in my section are going straight fool."

Angela smiled at Star and got started on the next drink order. They had an appearance by a well-known erotic movie star tonight, so the place was packed. "I'm pouring almost as fast as you all are ordering."

The sea of people parted and her boss, Z, walked up. Z was a big man, so most people got out of his way. His light brown skin glowed in the dim lights of the club, but he still wore dark shades and an all-black suit that made him look part gangster, part lethal businessman. Despite looking as if he'd kill you if you stepped on his new shoes, Z was a nice guy. He didn't allow the customers to abuse the women who worked at the club, accommodated any employees who had kids and never once caved to the frequent requests from customers to get a little more than a lap dance.

"Yo, Angel, we've got a big group coming to the VIP. I

want you to only work on those drinks," Z said in a deep, rumbling New York accent that cut through the music and cheers. He glanced at Diamond and Candy, the other bartenders. "You two handle the regular drinks. Don't let anyone wait for liquor, understand?"

The ladies all nodded. Angela barely suppressed her groan. Just serving VIP wasn't going to lighten her load. Men in VIP drank more and typically wanted their drinks yesterday.

"Who's in VIP, Z?" Angela called over the music.

"A bunch of ballers from the Gators. The usual fellas. Make sure you stay on those drinks."

Z walked away from the bar to walk through the crowd and check for any issues. Angela tried to ignore the quick beating of her heart. Members of the team came to Sweethearts often, but Isaiah wasn't typically part of the group. He'd only come in that night after they won the playoffs. She shouldn't get excited. They'd agreed to stay away from each other, and true to her word, she'd avoided him the rest of the week when she picked up Cory.

The increased buzz of excitement near the door announced the arrival of the players. Despite herself, Angela stood up on her toes to try and see over the crowd. She was ridiculous. Pour the drinks and forget about Isaiah.

She was about to look away when her eyes caught his. Her hand slipped and she nearly dropped the bottle of Patrón. Z was nice, but he'd have been pissed if she'd broken it. Her heart jumped. The corner of Isaiah's mouth tipped up in a smile. She bit her lower lip to keep from grinning. He was here.

Angela quickly looked away. She was not becoming his side chick. Nor was she going to demand he break up with the woman he'd been with off and on since college. She had no business getting all giddy because Isaiah was in her club.

She helped Diamond and Candy get ready to handle the floor before the drink orders came in from VIP. In the background she low-key watched the basketball players moving to their partitioned-off area. The first round of drink orders came two minutes after they were settled. She was working on that when the crowd parted, and suddenly Isaiah stood at the bar.

He was wearing a simple beige button-up and dark pants. When he leaned on the bar, the muscles in his arms flexed, begging her to touch and reminding her of the strength she'd felt the one time he'd held her. When they'd kissed. He watched her with a gleam in his eye that made her breasts heavy and her knees weak.

Angela walked over and placed her hands on the smooth surface of the bar, cocking her head to the side. "What are you doing here?"

His dark gaze moved to the sparkling wings on her back, then over her tight white tank top and short black skirt. "Kevin invited me."

Her nipples tightened when his gaze lingered on the heart charm resting right above her cleavage. Her thin bra and shirt wouldn't hide her response. "Can I get you a drink?" The noise in the club might hide the slight tremor in her voice.

"You look good."

She was told that all night, every night, but still her cheeks heated. She bit back another grin. Why was he here? She could ignore what she felt a lot easier when he wasn't standing in front of her. "I thought we were staying away from each other."

A muscle flexed in his jaw. Tension took over his shoulders. "I'm not with Bridget anymore."

The pounding of her heart increased to jackhammer proportions. Was she the reason? If she was, did it matter? He'd been with Bridget for years; now she was supposed to believe he was ready to give all that up for her?

She shrugged. "Am I supposed to care?" Points to her for sounding like she didn't when, despite her concerns, anticipation flooded her system.

His dark eyes met hers. Searched hers for something. "I'd like to think you cared."

"Isaiah Reynolds, wow, man, can I get your autograph?" one of the guys at the bar asked.

Angela accepted the interruption for what it was—an escape. She'd been a second away from saying she did care. *Crap.* What the hell did this mean? Was he free? Did he want to be with her?

One eager fan became a few others and soon Isaiah was thoroughly distracted. Angela focused on making the drinks for VIP before Z came over to ask what the holdup was.

A guy in her periphery waved a hand. She turned to get his order and froze. "Jerry?" Her stomach twisted.

Jerry, who couldn't handle his volunteers, from the office. Her face ached with the effort it took to smile. In the years she'd worked as an advocate, no one from the office had ever come into the club. She'd gotten complacent and stopped looking over her shoulder. She wasn't ashamed, but if Mr. Cooper found out, he'd use this as another example of her lack of commitment.

"Angela? I thought that was you." Jerry licked his lips as he looked her up and down. "What are you doing?"

"Serving drinks." Angela turned back to the printer and pulled out the next order of drinks from VIP. "What are you doing here?"

Dread coated every nerve. Jerry wasn't only known for

not being able to keep a handle on his volunteers, he also liked to stir up trouble in the office. There was no way he would walk out of here pretending he hadn't seen her.

"Serving drinks?" Jerry asked in disbelief. "That all you're serving?" He gawked at her chest. "Damn, girl. How much for a dance from you?" His friend chuckled.

Angela put her drinks on a tray with enough force to spill a few. Damn! Could tonight get worse? "I don't dance. Do you want a drink? Candy and Diamond can help you." She pointed to the other women. Though, from the red rims around his eyes and slight slur in his voice he probably didn't need another drink.

Jerry rubbed his hands together. "Not even a dance for my friend's birthday?"

"I don't dance. Now order or move on."

"Nah. I want to know why you act like you're too good to go out with me, but you're in here with all your goodies on display?"

Angela put a hand on her hip and glared at Jerry. Really? He had to be going back two years. She'd forgotten he'd even asked her out once upon a time. "It doesn't matter where I work or what I put on display. I don't have to go out with you."

Jerry's friend laughed again. Jerry's hands balled into fists and he scowled. "You aren't too good for me." He pulled cash out of his pocket and threw a few bills at her. "How much before you take off that top?"

Isaiah was instantly next to Jerry. He towered over the smaller man, his face hard and eyes angry. "Leave her alone."

Jerry didn't even look to see who stood beside him, he just continued to leer at Angela. "Why? That's what she's here for. How much?"

Angela fought back the urge to glare at Isaiah. She

didn't need him to step in on her behalf. She could take care of herself. "I wouldn't flash you for a million. Get out of my face, Jerry."

"You slu—" Jerry leaned over the counter.

Isaiah grabbed Jerry's shoulder and spun him around. Grabbing Jerry by the shirt, he hauled him up. "Call her a slut. I dare you."

"Isaiah, stop! He's drunk. I got this." Angela rushed out from behind the bar. The wings on her back snagged on a few patrons in her rush to get between the two mismatched men.

Jerry raised his arms in defeat. "I didn't mean any harm."

Angela tried to pull Isaiah off him, but his hard arms wouldn't budge. "Stop this."

Isaiah ignored her. "Apologize."

Cameras flashed while patrons watched. Damn! This was going from bad to worse. "Not necessary. Will you stop this?" She pulled on Isaiah's arm again.

The people parted and Z was making his way over. Even with his shades, she could feel his stare. He hated altercations in his club.

"All right, I'm sorry," Jerry squeaked.

A few other Gators members materialized at Isaiah's side. His glare didn't lessen. "Say it like you mean it."

"I'm sorry, Angela. I didn't mean any harm."

Isaiah pushed him back. Jerry stumbled into his friend. Z approached and looked between the two. "Is there a problem here?"

Isaiah shook his head. "None at all."

Jerry hurried away from the bar, though not before Angela caught one last sneer directed at her. Her body trembled with anger and embarrassment. She didn't need a white knight coming in to save her. She'd handled men much worse than Jerry in her years working here. "Z, I need a break."

His jaw clenched, but he nodded. "Five minutes. I've got the bar."

He knew she'd take ten. Isaiah touched her arm. She pushed him off and then squeezed through the crowd to the back. If she spoke to him, she'd curse him out in front of everyone. She didn't need him coming in to rescue her. She pushed through the double doors to the back hall, where the dressing rooms and Z's office were located.

The doors opened and closed again right behind her. She didn't have to guess who that was. She'd felt Isaiah's presence behind her as she stalked away from the bar. "I didn't need your help," she snapped over her shoulder.

"You wanted me to let him talk to you like that?" was his disbelieving reply.

Angela spun to face him, then stumbled back. He was directly behind her and she almost bumped into his chest. Anger and worry flashed in his dark eyes. Tension radiated off the muscles of his body. She could feel his emotions almost like a touch. She sucked in a breath and the smell of his cologne mixed desire with her own anger.

She glanced down the hall, thankfully empty at the moment, most of the dancers on the floor with such a large crowd. She opened a door to Bruno's office. The bouncer was also on the floor so she wouldn't have to worry about interruptions for a few minutes. Isaiah followed her in. She closed the door and glared at him.

"You aren't my man." Her voice trembled. "You can't come in here and act like I'm your woman."

"I can't just sit by and let someone talk to you like that. I wanted to help."

"I don't need your help. I can take care of myself. Your help only makes things worse."

Confusion covered his handsome face. "How?"

"I don't want you to lay claim on me when you're not free to do so. Don't step in and try to fix things for me when we both know you can't."

She snapped her mouth shut. Her chest heaved with ragged breaths. That was the problem. She could take care of herself, but a small part of her had liked it when he'd defended her. She couldn't remember the last time anyone, much less a guy, had stood up for her. She never wanted to be defended or shielded. She'd done all of that on her own. And enjoying his protection would only hurt more when he eventually went back to his superstar life and the woman he'd clung to for years.

Isaiah stepped forward. Angela backed up until her wings were crushed against the door. He pressed a hand on the door over her. "I'm free to do whatever I damn well choose. I told you Bridget and I are through."

"For how long?"

"For good."

"I didn't ask you to leave her."

"I couldn't stay with her knowing how I feel about you." His gaze devoured her. "Why are you still fighting this?"

She opened her mouth to say something noble, like *honor*, *independence* or *integrity*. His head lowered and her arguments faded to nothing. His body was a solid wall of firm muscle and masculine heat. The scent of his cologne was pure intoxication. He kept one hand on the wall, the other ran down her back, cupped her butt and pulled her flush against his body. Angela moaned. Her hands gripped his hips and held him close. The heat of his passion burned through her anger and ignited the fire she'd been craving since that first time they'd met.

The kiss started hard and heavy, then slowed into a

teasing seduction that had her soaking wet and aching. His lips and tongue slid over hers so thoroughly she could only whimper and lean in for more. She wanted—no, she needed more. Needed to rip off his clothes and feel his skin against hers.

Isaiah's hand caressed the length of her side down to the softness of her behind, then lifted one of her legs. The tips of his fingers brushed the underside of her thigh just below the hem of her short skirt. His hips pushed forward, bringing the full contact of his thick erection to the sweet heat between her thighs. Angela gasped. He repeated the move and her low moan filled the small office.

He lifted his head and met her gaze. The question in his eye was heightened by the slow creep of his fingers up her thigh toward her heated flesh. If he didn't touch her, she'd scream. She widened her legs. Surprise brightened his eyes. Then the dark flash of desire took over. Isaiah boldly caressed the sensitive sweetness of her sex through the lacy triangle of her thong.

Angela's lids drooped. Her head fell back. Warm lips pressed against her neck. His teeth nipped lightly, then his tongue soothed the slight pain. He was killing her with the slow steady strokes, driving her heart to its limit, taking her body on an erotic trip. She rotated her hips, bringing her fully against his fingers. Fingers weren't enough.

Angela jerked open his pants, her own fingers wrapping around him. Damn he was big. Isaiah groaned low and deep, then kissed her with an urgency that made her stroke him harder. Somewhere, in the very far back of her mind, she registered that this wasn't the right time, or the right place, but then his fingers pushed into her core and her mind surrendered.

Isaiah's other hand flew to his back pocket and produced a condom. Again the idea that maybe this was too soon popped in, but when he kissed her and his erection flexed in her palm, she didn't give a damn. His hands left her sex only to cover himself, then he bent and lifted her against the door. His mouth covered hers in a kiss so passionate it robbed her of everything but the ability to feel, to be in this exact moment. She wrapped her arms around his neck and her legs cinched his waist, holding him tight. Isaiah dipped low, his hand positioned, and he straightened and filled her inch by thick inch.

Her arms and legs tightened around him. His strong arms jerked her closer and he slid deeper and harder with each thrust. Angela's mouth fell open in silent cries. The pleasure was so intense she couldn't even vocalize how good he felt inside her. She gripped the back of his head and met his thrusts with eager pulses of her own. The door vibrated behind her, and the sounds of her harsh breaths met with Isaiah's own grunts of pleasure. He bit his lower lip and squeezed her tight.

The quivers of her orgasm started. She wasn't ready. She wanted this to last longer, to hold him longer. But he probably sensed how close she was, and increased his pace. Angela's body shattered into a thousand threads of ecstasy. She buried her face in his neck, then bit down on his shoulder to stop herself from crying out for the world to hear. She felt the hard pulses of his own release. He pushed her harder against the door and slapped one hand against the solid wood.

They broke apart slowly. He looked at her as if he wanted her again, and an aftershock of need went through her. She looked away quickly and pulled down her skirt. If she kept his gaze she'd be back against the door. His cell phone chimed. Isaiah pulled up his pants, but didn't fasten them. He took out the phone, frowned and turned his back.

Curious, Angela moved beside him to see. A text from Bridget. He pressed the button on the side and quickly darkened the screen.

"Bathroom?"

"Why is she texting you?" Angela heard the accusation in her voice, but didn't care.

"She wants to talk."

"Are you two really over?" Or was Angela just a fun stopover during his break from Bridget. Tendrils of doubt crept across her brain like a weed. He'd come here tonight and said he was free, but he just happened to have a condom ready in his back pocket? Isaiah said he wasn't a player, but the guys who came to Sweethearts with condoms in their pockets came because they expected more than a dance.

"For me it is. She thinks this is just another temporary split." He sounded tired, exasperated even.

Angela didn't buy it. For the second time, Isaiah made her feel like he'd been playing with her. "The bathroom is down the hall to the right." He reached for her and she backed away. "I won't be your side piece. This won't happen again." She slipped through the door and out into the hall. A couple of the dancers hurried away from the door. Their whispers and giggles followed as they went back to the main floor.

"Damn!" she muttered. Not only had she been played for a fool, but she'd also been caught. Z had a strict rule of no sex with clients. Especially not in his club. Shit, damn and boy was she screwed.

Her cheeks burned and she quickly rushed to the ladies' room before Isaiah came out. She pulled the heart-shaped diffuser charm on her necklace to her nose to fill her nostrils with lavender, but all she smelled was Isaiah's cologne. She groaned and splashed water on her face. Walking away from him was the right decision. She was in a ton of trouble after tonight. So how come all she wanted to do was find Isaiah and repeat their mistake?

Chapter 14

One week from the night at the club, and Angela was sure she'd have a mental breakdown. Thank heaven it was Friday. Between working late all week, walking on pins and needles waiting for Jerry to drop the bomb about seeing her at Sweethearts and playing the memory of having sex with Isaiah on repeat, she was more than ready for the weekend and a glass of wine. Maybe three.

They weren't training on Fridays so she was able to slip out of the office right before five. A few coworkers smiled and waved, but no one stopped her to talk, avoided her gaze, or whispered behind their hands. She was tempted to believe Jerry was going to let everything that happened the week before go, but she wasn't that naive. He wouldn't be that nasty to her only to drop everything. Which meant her pins-and-needles walk was going to last over the weekend.

The back of her neck prickled when she got to her car. She looked over her shoulder and spotted Jerry and a few people from his section walking out of the office. They hadn't been in the same training group so she hadn't seen him much during the week. Now, he met her eye, throwing her a smug smile. Angela's stomach constricted but she responded to the look with a glower. She should have said something to Tamara, but figured Jerry would have said something first. No more waiting the jerk out; she'd call Tamara over the weekend and give her a heads-up.

With one last glare at Jerry, she got into her car, started the engine and turned the air-conditioning on full blast. She rolled down the windows until the air-conditioning conquered the excessive heat inside her car.

She had to pick up Cory by six o'clock today. The Gators had taken the kids to the beach for a barbecue. The staff had made it very clear that all kids needed to be picked up by six, no excuses since they weren't at the center.

She'd worked late all week and had informed Keri that either Vicki or Nate would pick up Cory. A cop-out to avoid Isaiah, but she needed breathing room. She and Cory, on the other hand, had come to a truce. He'd have a babysitter until he was fourteen at the end of the summer. But he wouldn't need one tonight because Angela would be picking him up, and she knew there was a good chance she'd see Isaiah. Her hands gripped the steering wheel. Isaiah didn't have her number so she hadn't expected a call, or for him to send a message via Cory. That didn't make it easier to move on from what happened, or keep her mind from asking pointless questions she certainly wasn't going to ask Cory about. Was Isaiah back with Bridget? Had he thought of her? Did he really only come to the club that night to sleep with her? The questions were pointless because they changed nothing. If anything, they just left her feeling more confused.

When she arrived at the beach barbecue, her heart jumped nervously. She may have told Isaiah they wouldn't be repeating what happened, but that didn't stop the tingle of anticipation over the possibility of seeing him again. Or prevent her mind from remembering his kiss, his fingers against her slick folds, the long length of him filling her, or the explosion of pleasure he'd given her.

Angela groaned and turned off the engine. "Be strong, girl," she mumbled and got out of the car.

Friday was casual day in the office so she usually wore jeans. But today she'd opted for a sleeveless, sage, jersey-knit dress that hugged her body like a lover, paired with gold sandals. She took off the white blazer she'd worn to the office, ran her fingers through her hair and slipped on a coat of lip gloss before heading down to the beach. Looking good when she pretended to not want him wasn't a terrible idea.

She crossed the boardwalk and spotted the group from the camp. They'd popped up a tent and a group of kids and adults were playing volleyball nearby. She walked closer and spotted Cory among those playing, a huge smile on his face. He appeared to be having a blast. She scanned the rest of the players and her mouth went dry.

Isaiah was in the game, too. Shirtless. The afternoon sun glistened on chest and abs, which were clearly sculpted by angels. Hair covered his chest and trailed down his body into the waistband of his swim trunks—a trail she desperately wanted to follow. She licked her lip, tried to swallow, but nothing happened. Sweat popped along her body and not from the warmth of the sun. Her nipples tightened and heat settled heavily between her thighs.

Stay away. You're supposed to stay away from him.

Why did he have to look so damn fine?

He looked up and caught her eye, then froze in the middle of the field. Her fingers itched to play over every inch of his bared flesh. The lure was so strong she took a step toward him before common sense prevailed. She played with the charm on her necklace, her hands needing to touch something. Isaiah's gaze dipped to her hand above her cleavage. Despite the distance, she saw the heavy breath he took as his gaze sharpened. Bad move.

The volleyball hit the side of his head. The spell was broken. The players on his team groaned, the players on the other team laughed.

"That's game," Cory called. He was playing against Isaiah. "We won!"

Angela shook her head and forced her greedy gaze away from Isaiah's beautiful body. Why was she staying away from him again?

You're a pit stop on his way back to the girl he's kept dangling for years. The one who's only in town now because he asked her to come.

Yes, that's right. She wasn't playing side chick.

The teams got together to congratulate the winners. Cory saw her and waved. She walked over to Keri, chitchatted about the activities for the last few days of camp and signed out Cory.

"Having Cory in the camp has been great," Keri said. "Even if there were some touchy moments."

Angela frowned. "Touchy moments? Has he given you any problems?"

Keri's grin turned sly. "Not Cory. I'm hoping you and Isaiah can make it one more week."

Angela's face heated. "Nothing happened." At the camp anyway. "I didn't approach him or ask for anything." She didn't want Keri to think she'd used this opportunity to get anything from the players.

"I know. He told me the same thing. But you two could cause fires when you see each other. Let's just say, I hope you can continue to hold out a little longer. I really don't want to have to dismiss Cory. But… I also can't really get angry when I see a relationship blossom. What can I say? I'm a bit of a romantic." Keri winked. "Good luck. He's a good one."

Before Angela could correct her and say nothing would happen between her and Isaiah, another parent walked up to sign out their kid. Keeping her gaze away from Isaiah's naked chest, Angela searched the crowd and found Cory gathering his things from a pile at the other end of the tent. She walked over to him.

"Well, how was the beach barbecue?" she asked.

Cory's grin split his face. "Awesome. Did you see we beat Isaiah's team in volleyball?"

"I did. Great job." The back of her neck prickled. This time she was filled with a jolt of excitement, as opposed to trepidation. She didn't have to turn to know the man who watched her. "Ready to go?" She hoped Cory didn't pick up on the note of desperation in her voice. She had to get out of here.

"Yeah, just a second. I wrote something for Denise." He gave her a sheepish smile. "I didn't want to give it to her at the start of the day and give the guys a chance to see. Let me take it to her now."

"Okay, but hurry."

Cory nodded, then ran across the sand to a group of kids standing by the volleyball net. He said a few words to Denise and the two of them separated from the group. *Please let him hurry up so we can leave before I jump Isaiah.*

"Hello, Angel."

Too late. Isaiah's voice warmed her like the sun's rays. She slowly turned to face him. Up close, half-naked Isaiah was worse than far away. She'd touched that chest. Felt the softness of his skin over the hardness of muscle. She dragged her eyes up from his abs and chest to the seductive heat in his eyes.

"Good game." It was a dumb statement, but she didn't know what else to say.

"You look beautiful." His voice held a note she was afraid to believe was wonder.

"Don't. I thought I was clear—"

He took a step forward. The smell of sweat, cologne and his underlying scent made her body tremble. "I didn't lie. Bridget and I are done."

"You also haven't called me." Damn, did she have to sound so hurt? She didn't want him to see she was hurting.

"I don't have your number and asking Cory or Keri was out of the question. I'd hoped to catch you this week."

"I had to work late."

"I would have watched Cory."

Her eyes snapped to his. "I don't need you to watch him. I had it covered. We don't need to get attached to you."

"I'm already attached to you, Angela," he said softly, hesitantly. If the statement had been bold or demanding she would have been able to defend herself. When he sounded just as confused and swept away as she felt, she had no defense. Only yearning.

"Isaiah, I…" She didn't know how to respond. She was attached to him, too, but to tell him that gave him too much power over her heart. She wasn't ready to give him that.

His lips lifted in a smile. "It's funny. I couldn't forget you after we met that first time. This camp was a coincidence that brought us back together. I don't want to forget about you. I don't want to pretend to be happy with the arrangement Bridget and I had." He took her hand in his. "I don't want any obstacles to stop us from being together."

As much as she wanted to give in and say yes, pessimism bubbled up. "I don't want to be your rebound, or an intermission in your relationship with her. Don't come for me if you don't really want to be with me."

The smile on his face turned her legs to seawater. "I'm coming for you, not to play with you, but to leave absolutely no doubt in your mind that I want you to be mine."

She couldn't stop her own smile from coming.

She had to smile otherwise she'd jump on him, wrap her arms around his neck, her legs around his waist, and scream for him to take her then and there. Which would force Keri to kick out Cory. "What about camp? Cory will get kicked out."

"There's a week left and I'll talk to Keri. I won't let him get kicked out over this."

"But…"

"No buts. We're doing this." He looked a little unsure. "You do want to do this, right?"

More than anything. "I guess we should officially go on a date first."

His grin made her happiness shine brighter than the sun. "When?" he asked in a voice that said yesterday.

"Tonight."

Isaiah squeezed her hand. "I'll pick you up at eight."

Isaiah knocked on Angela's door at exactly eight o'clock. He anxiously tugged on his bow tie. He'd rushed home, showered and changed in record time. Maybe he should have waited to take her out until next week, when camp officially ended, but he didn't want to go another day now that he was truly free to be with Angela.

He adjusted his bow tie one last time, then dropped his hands to his sides. He wanted their first date to be memorable so he'd called in a few favors to be sure. Her door opened and he sucked in a breath. Angela looked every bit the angel he'd called her. A fitted emerald green dress draped seductively over her full breasts and hips. Strappy silver heels added some height; they'd fit together even better than before because of those. A berry-colored gloss enhanced already kissable lips, and her thick hair was pulled to the side in a loose but sexy twist.

"Damn," he whispered, taking her in from head to toe.

Her smile made him think he'd embarrassed her. She smoothed her hand over her hair and glanced away. "You look nice, too. I like the bow tie."

"Kinda my thing." The guys teased him for the preppy look, but he didn't care. His dad preferred bow ties and used to make him and his brother wear them. Isaiah liked the look and had continued to make them his signature style.

"I know. That's why I like it."

His chest puffed up. She could say she liked his socks and he'd be just as happy.

Cory popped out from behind Angela and waved. "Hey, Isaiah."

Isaiah waved back. "Hey, Cory. I promise to get her home at a decent time."

Cory laughed. "Stay out late. That way I can stay out when I start going on dates."

Angela rolled her eyes. "You still won't get to stay out late. I'm grown." She waved Isaiah in. "I need to grab a few things. Can you wait a second?"

"Sure." He followed her in. Her apartment was small but nice. She'd decorated with neutral furniture, but added some color with a few dark blue pillows and throws.

A tall black guy sat on her couch with a laptop on

his lap. He glanced up at Isaiah, pushed the laptop aside and stood.

Angela pointed to him. "Nate, this is Isaiah. Isaiah, this is Nate, my neighbor and babysitter."

Cory groaned. "I don't need a babysitter."

Angela waved her hand. "Fine, teen-sitter. I'll be right back." She went down a hall that Isaiah assumed led to her bedroom.

He glanced back at Nate. Recognized him as the guy who'd picked up Cory a few days that week. Nate was shorter than Isaiah by a few inches, wore a Star Wars T-shirt, pants that were scraped up enough to be considered trendy and frantically chewed gum while grinning at Isaiah.

"It's so great to meet you." Nate rushed forward and held out his hand. "I'm a huge fan. Cory and I have talked almost every day about the things you're teaching them in camp. I think it's awesome what you all do for the kids."

Isaiah shook Nate's hand and relaxed a little. He'd wondered if the teen-sitter would try to flex and stake a claim on Angela. "The camp is one of the best parts of the year. Cory is a real talented kid."

Nate nodded. "Are you excited about the new season? You start practice pretty soon, right?"

Isaiah and Nate talked about the Gators' expectations for the upcoming season while they waited for Angela. Cory half contributed, but spent more time texting on his phone. Nate didn't show a hint of jealousy or bad intentions while they talked, which was cool. Isaiah didn't want to get into a fight for dominance with Nate, but he wouldn't be fully comfortable until he was sure Nate wasn't hanging in Angela's "friend zone" with the hopes of landing her in bed.

Angela came back out and Isaiah knew he had to look

enthralled. His cheeks hurt he smiled so hard and he was even forcing himself to hold back. This was his problem; he jumped headfirst into things. The way Angela made him feel had him more than willing to skip the getting-to-know-you phase.

"Ready?" she asked.

"More than ready."

Nate grinned at them. "Stay out as late as you want. Cory and I are going to make it to the end of the new *Call of Duty* game."

"I'm going to lead the team," Cory said, not looking up from his phone.

They said their goodbyes and Isaiah led Angela out to his car. "So…what's up with Nate?"

She threw him a questioning glance. "What do you mean?"

"Okay, I'm going to be real. I don't know many guys who're willing to babysit."

She chuckled. "Don't worry. He has free time and I pay him to play video games and make sure Cory doesn't burn down the place. He also has a girlfriend that I adore."

He opened the passenger-side door. "Cool."

She rolled her eyes and grinned. "Glad you approve," her voice was teasing. She slid into the seat.

Isaiah nodded and closed the door. She paid Nate and he had a girlfriend. That was good. He really was a baby-sitter and not just trying to make himself invaluable in her life.

"Where are we going?" she asked after he got in the driver's seat.

"I'm going to show you the city like you've never seen it before."

She raised an eyebrow. "I grew up here, so there aren't many ways I haven't seen the city."

"Say that again at the end of the night."

Chapter 15

"Oh, my God! That was incredible!" Angela said after she and Isaiah got off the helicopter and were back in his car.

He hadn't lied. He'd shown her the city in a way she hadn't seen before. Via helicopter they'd toured everything from the river to the sea, and even caught a glimpse of a gorgeous sunset before returning to the helicopter pad.

He glanced away from the road and smiled at her. "I'm glad you liked it. But we're not through."

"What's next?" She could barely hide her excitement—not that she wanted to.

"I hope you're hungry."

He took her to a seafood restaurant that overlooked the ocean. They had a private balcony all to themselves. The soft sounds of jazz drifted out from the inside of the restaurant while their conversation flowed easily, covering his childhood and time playing basketball in college. Hearing about his love for his family made her yearn for the family she'd lost.

"I remember what that feels like," she said, staring into the candle on the table.

"What's that?"

"Being surrounded by the love of your family."

Concern filled his dark gaze. "It's just a memory?"

"My parents died in a car crash when I was thirteen. That's why my aunt took in me and my brother."

Isaiah dropped his hand over hers, a warm and comforting gesture that soothed some of her pain of the memory. "That must've been hard, losing both of them like that."

She took a shaky breath, remembering the sadness, fear and concern of starting a new life in her aunt's home. "We didn't know my aunt that well. I appreciate what she did by taking us in, but she never let us forget that we owed her for doing so. If we talked too loud, asked for seconds at dinner, or needed school supplies, she'd remind us she could easily drop us off at the child welfare office and never look back. She viewed us as a burden and made sure we knew it."

Isaiah's body went rigid, his hand on hers tightening slightly. "Why did she agree to be your guardian only to take it out on you and your brother?"

"Simple—money. She took everything our parents left for us." The pain of her aunt's betrayal was a blow she hadn't expected to recover from.

"Could she do that?" Anger filled Isaiah's voice.

"That's what we wondered. I went to a lawyer at the time. It would've taken money I didn't have to sue her in the hopes of getting anything back."

"I know a lawyer who can help."

Angela shook her head. She'd survived and thrived. She wanted nothing more to do with her aunt. "No, that was years ago. Finding out my college fund was gone is one of the reasons I became a bartender. The tips helped pay my way through college."

"You're out of college now." His tone implied she didn't need to work the bar anymore.

"I'm out of undergrad. I've worked with the child advocacy office for four years. When I asked my boss what would it take to become a manager, she mentioned the position requires a master's degree. I've got one more semester and then I'm done."

His eyes brightened with admiration. "That's pretty big."

"I know. A part of me can't wait. The other part of me won't know what to do with myself. I would have been done sooner, but I opted out of summer school because of Cory."

He leaned forward on the table and threaded his fingers through hers. The little claim made her feel giddy. The candlelight danced in the dark pools of his eyes. His tailored jacket perfectly fit his strong arms. She wanted those arms around her again.

"Do you mind telling me what happened with your brother?"

She sighed and reached for the champagne flute with her other hand. "I decided to work hard to make the money I needed. His chosen method was to steal it. He worked for the water department, skimmed funds off the top of bills."

Isaiah's eyes widened. "That was your brother? I remember seeing that on the news a few months back."

"Yep, my brother. Shortly after he went to jail, Cory's mom decided she wasn't giving up her dream to be a stage star. She left Cory with me and ran to New York."

"She didn't have family that could've taken him?"

"Her family is a lot like my aunt. I know what it feels like to be unwanted. I won't let Cory feel that way. I don't want any kid to feel that way. It's why I love my job. Why

I really hope what happened the other day doesn't come back and screw me over."

"That Jerry guy." Isaiah's voice hardened on her co-worker's name. "You know him?"

"He works in my office. I had a feeling he'd go back and tell the director about my job, but he didn't. Which means he's hoping to spring it at the worst time."

"Would that be a major problem?"

His thumb ran back and forth over her fingers, sending flutters over her body. "The director is very conservative. My direct supervisor knows I tend bar at Sweethearts and she's willing to ignore that. If the director found out, he may not be as understanding."

"But you don't dance." He said that as if it was a saving grace. Did he have a problem with her working there?

"Doesn't matter. He wants all the advocates to be pillars of morality. Working at a strip club won't exactly meet that requirement."

Isaiah considered her words. He sat up straight but didn't let go of her hand. "What would make you quit? If staying there threatens your job with the agency?"

"Winning the lottery." She teased, then laughed. "I need the money to pay for graduate school. I have no student loan debt so far. I want to keep it that way."

She couldn't tell if that answer pleased or bothered him. "What are you going to do about Jerry?"

"Jerry probably didn't say anything because he doesn't want to admit being there. I'm going to my boss about what happened instead of waiting to see if he'll drop the bomb." The idea of the upcoming confrontation made her stomach ache. Tonight wasn't the night for worries. "I don't want to talk about work anymore."

"Fine with me. This is a date." Isaiah stood and held out his hand. "Dance with me."

"Are you serious?"

"I want to hold you again." He said it so seriously her heart constricted.

She put her hand in his. He pulled her up and wrapped her in his strong embrace. One hand ran up and down her back; the fingers of his other hand entwined with hers. With the slightest hint of pressure, he brought her closer. The contact brought back memories of the way he'd held her against the door. The deep strokes that had stolen her breath. He lowered his head to the crook of her neck and inhaled deeply.

She wanted to hold him, too. Her hand slid up and cupped the back of his neck. Turning her head, she pressed a kiss to his cheek. Isaiah straightened and brought their joined hands to rest on his chest.

"I also want to make love to you again." The low growl in his voice was seduction incarnate.

Her stomach tightened. Desire spread its enticing warmth through her every cell. She wanted to strip him naked and jump him again. "Is that what you're calling what happened?" She tried to tease, but sounded breathless. How did he make her ability to control herself fly away as if on a breeze? "Some guys would call it something else."

"If I wanted to call what happened between us anything else, I would have. I want to make love to you again." He lowered his head and his lips brushed her ears. "Your bed or mine?"

His lips closed lightly over the tip of her ear. A tremble shot up and through her. His heart pounded beneath their joined hands, working just as hard as hers. Mingled in with his bold words and gaze was a hint of nervous-

ness. He felt just as blown away by this as she did, a realization that calmed her own nerves and smashed any
hesitation she may have felt.

"Yours."

Chapter 16

The last time Isaiah had been this nervous was when the first recruiter came to one of his basketball games. His heart pumped as if it was the last game in the finals and anticipation coursed through him in waves. The other night at the club had been spontaneous and completely out of character for him, but he didn't regret it at all. The wild feelings Angela stirred in him were scary. He wasn't one to back away from fear, but he'd never been good at suave and seductive. The awkward teenager he once was hovered right under the surface as they walked into his place.

"Would you like a drink?" he asked.

Angela toyed with the loose twist of her hair, then dropped her hand to play with the circular charm resting right above her cleavage. She met his gaze through thick lashes and her smile turned his blood to lava. "I'm not thirsty." Her voice was soft and flirty.

His semihard cock tightened even more. He regulated his breathing instead of panting like he wanted to. Hell, he wanted to grab her, throw her over his shoulder and run to his bedroom. But that would be a bit too eager.

He held out a hand and she slipped hers in his. He took

a deep breath. He was a grown man. He definitely wasn't a virgin. He just had to calm down and take things slow.

He pulled her forward and kissed her softly. She pressed closer until her full breasts cushioned his chest. Her lips clung to his. She tasted like wine and the fruity flavor of her lip gloss. He could sip from her forever. Instead he eased back before he lifted her up and took her against the front door.

"Would you like to go to my room?" Good. He sounded calm and in control. Because his body was wound tight with need.

She nodded and licked her full lips. "Yes," she said in a breathless tone.

Isaiah squeezed her hand slightly and led her upstairs. While she took in his bedroom, he slipped out his cell phone. He pulled up a love-songs playlist and music flowed from the Bluetooth speakers in his ceiling.

Angela looked up, then back at him with a smile. "Smooth. I love this song."

He nodded appreciatively before putting the phone on his dresser. Otherwise she'd see the full-on relief in his face. He'd worried she'd find the move cheesy.

When he turned back and met her gaze, Angela's chest rose with a deep breath. She pulled her thick lower lip between her teeth and watched him, her expression awash with coy desire. She was beautiful, sexy and all his. Angela, in his bedroom, in his life; this was right. His heart hammered. He was falling hard for her. He didn't want his eagerness to make her run, but he'd made the right decision. He wanted Angela in his life permanently.

He took his time walking back to her. The urge to run back and lift her against him a physical throb. Her breathing increased as he got closer, the pulse in her neck a fast beat. Threading their fingers together, he brought her into his arms and moved to the rhythm of "It Won't Stop" by Sevyn Streeter coming through the speakers.

"Last time things were rushed." He brought their entangled hands to his chest. The other slid from her shoulders down the curve of her back to rest right above her round behind. "I don't want to rush tonight."

Angela's eyes warmed to dark pools he wanted to drown in. Her hand gripped the back of his shirt and she nodded quickly. They danced slowly, their bodies swaying to the beat. Her tantalizing breasts brushed against his chest. Thighs that he'd barely gotten to appreciate previously bumped into his. The tension of his arousal grew until Isaiah thought his body, one part in particular, might explode.

His fingers found the zipper to her dress and eased it down. Angela's breath hitched and she met his eyes. He rested his hands on her shoulders, then pushed the dress down. With a slight shimmy, the material fell to the floor.

Angela kicked the dress aside, then brought all her luscious curves back to his arms. He ran his hands up and down her sides, committing the lines of her body and smooth skin to memory. She tugged on the bow tie. The pressure of the accessory released, and she tossed it aside. Then, slowly, she unbuttoned and removed his shirt. Soft lips kissed his chest, light as a feather but causing a rumble strong enough to weaken his knees. He gripped her hips, forced her closer. Slow. He was going slow. The tip of Angela's tongue flicked his nipple. He gasped. To hell with going slow. Every touch of her tongue was answered with a pulse of his dick.

He unhooked her bra. Were his fingers trembling? He didn't care. The bra was gone and he held the weight of her breasts in his hands, ran his thumbs over the hard tips, relished in her low moan and the way her back arched.

He had to taste her. A tug on his waistband, then Angela had his pants unfastened. Her hand slipped into his boxers and wrapped around him.

He sucked in air through clenched teeth. Her lips were back on his chest while her hands brought him to every level of heaven imaginable. If she didn't stop, he'd embarrass himself.

Lowering to his knees, Isaiah slipped her panties down at the same time. Her cute little belly button called to him. The scent of her arousal made his mouth water. His erection harder. He kissed her stomach and ran his fingers through the slick heat of her sex. Angela cried out softly. Her hand clutched his shoulder. He couldn't hold back, leaned in, and tasted her sweetness. Angela gripped the back of his head and moaned softly. The taste and feel of her as something he'd never forget.

He kissed her intimately until her legs trembled, and her breath became short gasps. Isaiah stood, lifted her nearly limp body, and placed her gently on his bed. He grabbed protection from the nightstand, covered himself, then covered her beautiful body with his. As he slid into her, his entire body shuddered from the pleasure. He could stay there all night, forever. Like an explorer who'd discovered a hidden treasure, excitement, satisfaction and intense happiness flowed through him. Keeping pace with the love songs playing in the room, he made love to her slowly. Rhythmically. Her moans— so soft and feminine—were driving him wild. Deeper, harder, more. The words pounded with his pulse. His control was slipping. Sliding a hand between them, he teased her pearl. Angela's head pressed into the mattress, her body squeezing him tight. The shudder of her orgasm was the most beautiful thing he'd ever seen and pushed him over the edge.

He wanted to collapse on top of her after, but rolled over onto his back. Angela snuggled up against his side and he held her close. He must have dozed because he jerked awake minutes later. Angela lifted her head and her lips curled in a small smile.

"It's getting late. I should go home." She sounded as disappointed as he felt.

"Give me a second and I'll take you." He dragged himself out of the bed and into the bathroom to clean up. When he returned, she was still in the bed. Isaiah slipped between the sheets and Angela moved on top of him.

He ran his hands over her thighs and grinned at her. "Damn, you're sexy as hell."

"So are you." She ran her fingers over his chest.

Something tightened in his chest. His smile drifted as everything he was feeling overwhelmed him. "I'm going to want you here every night."

Surprise flashed in her eyes. Isaiah wished he could take the words back. Not cool to reveal he was so addicted to her already.

Her grin turned wicked. "Then let me give you something to remember on the nights I'm not here."

Before he could be thankful she hadn't explored his admission, Angela ducked between the covers. Her warm lips closed over him. Isaiah gripped the sheets. Remember her only at night? He was going to remember her every moment of every day.

Chapter 17

Angela and Vicki sipped coffee in the mall food court that Saturday afternoon. Cory had wanted to meet Denise at the mall, and since she wasn't quite ready to drop him off and leave him alone despite him insisting that she could, Angela had woken up Vicki and asked her to meet her there. She wanted the company, but what she really needed was to talk to someone about what happened with Isaiah.

She'd just given Vicki an overview of their fantastic date, skimming through the really good parts and ending with his declaration of wanting her over every night. She wanted to be with him every night, too. Which was crazy because they'd just started dating. Vicki was jaded enough to be able to see through Angela's sunshine-and-roses point of view and tell her to be careful.

Vicki pursued her lips and shook her head. "Girl, you know you can't believe what a man tells you in bed. Especially before, during, or after sex. Don't read anything in to that."

Vicki played with the straw in her double expresso macchiato. She'd worked the night before and typically slept in late. Even though she hated the mall, she'd thrown on a pair of light green shorts and a matching tank, popped her hair into a ponytail and met Angela. Angela appreciated Vicki's show of friendship.

"I know," Angela said in an exaggerated tone. "I'm reading too much into this, right? It's because I like him so much. I haven't liked a guy like this since…" She tried to remember.

Vicki rolled her eyes. "Since never. At least not while I've known you."

They'd known each other since Angela first began working at Sweethearts. "I've liked guys. I just haven't really been feeling one. I meet guys at the day job and they're either volunteers I can't get involved with or the deadbeat parents I'm helping. The guys who hit on me at the club…you know you can't believe the feelings you get from the guys we meet at the club."

Which was why she'd gone so long without a serious relationship, but was Isaiah the right guy to get serious with?

"What makes him any different from the other guys we meet?" Vicki asked. "Most of them come to the club with condoms in their pockets, ready to get laid."

Vicki was examining her nails so she missed Angela's wince. Hadn't Isaiah done the same thing? Sure, he said his teammate always gave them out to the fellas when they went to clubs, but that didn't mean he really hadn't come expecting more than just to tell her he was done with Bridget—or worse, hook up with someone else.

"How many people know?" Angela asked.

"Everyone." Vicki met her gaze. "You know Sapphire and Juicy were listening on the other side of the door, and they are the two most hating heifers at Sweethearts. They've been trying to get one of those players to ask them home for months. Only to have the *bartender* land one?"

She said bartender as if it was unheard of, but Angela didn't take offense. The bartenders weren't what the men came to Sweethearts for and she knew it. She ran a hand over her face. This wasn't going to be good.

"Did Bruno say what Z is going to do?" Z had a strict policy against the women in the club doing anything with the patrons on club property. That's how he was able to say his place was classy, unlike some other clubs.

"Nope. He's saying he doesn't believe it, but I think that's because he doesn't want to fire you. So, get your story straight before tonight." Angela was on the schedule for tonight and she wasn't looking forward to facing Z. She knew she couldn't lie to him, but she also couldn't afford to lose her job right before the last semester.

"I hope Isaiah means what he's telling you. That'll help if you're together and not just hooking up," Vicki said.

Angela sighed and sipped the creamy caramel Frappuccino. "He says all the right things. Sometimes I think he's just as excited and nervous about our relationship as I am."

Vicki raised an eyebrow. "Angela, he's a professional basketball player. The guy probably has women coming at him constantly. I doubt he's shy about how to be with a woman."

"But he's not one of the ones in the news all the time with a different woman on his arm. He doesn't come across as a dog."

"I'll agree with you on that." Vicki reached over and rubbed Angela's arm. "Look, I'm not telling you to not sleep with him. I mean…that would be crazy. Just take things slow. Don't get yourself in too deep. He did just break up with the perfect woman his family loves."

"So?"

"Family pressure is a bitch, especially a family like

his. I bet you money they're going to give him a hard time and they're going to want to examine you. If he's as into you as you think, they're going to wonder what magic spell you pulled out of your punanny—" she leaned back and pointed down "—that made him give up years of off and on with Ms. Wonderful to be with you." Vicki tilted her head and gave a know-what-I'm-saying look that Angela couldn't ignore.

"If anything they'll see I'm falling way too hard and fast for Isaiah and feel sorry for me."

Vicki laughed, but it wasn't unkind. "Sure. Wealthy privileged folks always look for the good side of the underdog."

Angela's phone vibrated on the table. "Maybe Cory is ready to go," she said. Vicki snorted and Angela grinned. She picked up the phone, but the call was from Nate.

"Hey, Nate, what's going on?"

"One of the guys who works at the local station mentioned an exposé he and his team are working on," Nate said in a grim voice.

"Okay," Angela said warily. "What kind of exposé and why are you telling me?" She took a sip of her drink.

"They're talking about what really happens at local strip clubs. That men don't just get dances there. He mentioned Sweethearts and that they have witnesses who can vouch for the fact that Gators players come in and can, and I quote, 'have sex with any of the girls—even the bartenders—in the back offices.'"

Angela choked. The burn as the caramel-flavored coffee skipped her throat and skidded down her windpipe brought tears to her eyes. She coughed uncontrollably. While mortification stole what little air she could take in. Vicki was up and around their table in an instant. She pounded on Angela's back.

"I'm okay," Angela wheezed and held up a hand. Vicki stopped pounding but she placed a hand on Angela's shoulder.

"I really hope that coughing fit is because you're outraged and not because you're surprised you were caught," Nate said.

Angela cleared her throat but her stomach churned. Her lunch may not stay down. "Are you sure?"

"I'm very sure. They've been working the story for months and he said they got this latest tip on yesterday. Including cell phone recordings."

"Did they give names?" Angela asked.

"The name Angel was mentioned," Nate said grimly.

Angela dropped her head into her hand. "Sweet Jesus."

Vicki's hand tightened on her shoulder. "What?"

She couldn't answer that right now. "This has the potential to be terrible. I could lose my job at the advocacy center." Could? No, she *would* lose her job if the director got word of this.

"I just thought you needed the heads-up. You might want to tell Isaiah, too. This won't be good with the season starting up."

Angela nodded even though Nate couldn't see. "I will. Thanks for telling me. Did he say when the story would air?"

"Next week. They're going to start running promos for it this weekend."

Angela cursed, not at Nate, but in general. She then thanked him again and got off the phone. Vicki watched her with wary eyes. Angela took a deep breath and told her what Nate had said. Vicki sat heavily on the seat next to Angela.

"This is going to suck for the club."

Angela tugged on the charm around her neck. She

brought it to her nose and breathed in the lavender scent, but her stomach still churned. "I can't believe this is happening."

"You better call Z. He shouldn't be blindsided with this."

Anegala nodded. But then another thought iced her over. What if Cory saw the story? He thought it was cool for Angela to date Isaiah, but the news wasn't interested in the hows or whys of what happened. They would make it sound sordid and dirty. He didn't need this embarrassment right after his parents abandoned him. She picked up her phone with shaky hands to call Z. Right now she had to trust in her feelings for Isaiah, because if he wasn't as serious about her as he let her believe, then she'd succumbed to her heart for nothing but a whole lot of pain.

Chapter 18

Although the first practice didn't start until two weeks after the summer camp ended, Isaiah met up with Will, Kevin and Jacobe at the Gators' auditorium to work out and prepare for the start of the season. He hadn't seen Jacobe much this summer. After his friend had proposed to his girlfriend, he'd spent a lot of his free time with her. Isaiah didn't begrudge him. Jacobe had gone through some rough stuff with unfaithful women in the past and deserved happiness.

He and the guys worked out for a few hours, ran a few drills for another hour and were getting dressed in the locker room when Isaiah finally told them about Angela.

Kevin's eyes widened and he put his fist over his open mouth. "Damn! You really let Bridget go? For good?"

Isaiah nodded. "I did."

Will shook his head. "For a stripper?" His voice said he didn't believe it.

"She's not a stripper, she's a bartender," Isaiah said, defending Angela.

"In a strip club," Will replied. He had one foot on the bench in the locker room and was tying the laces on his sneakers.

"She's also a child advocate—she'll have a master's

degree at the end of one more semester and she took in her nephew when his parents ditched him. She's more than a bartender at a strip club."

Kevin's eyes narrowed. "Wait? Did she give you some sob story? You know you can't believe the sad tales these women out here give you. They're always looking for a come-up." He pulled a black T-shirt out of his locker and covered his tattooed chest with it.

"She didn't give a sob story. She's not trying to get something out of me," Isaiah said with more patience than he felt. Only because he understood his friend's concerns did he not let his frustration show. Angela was more than where she worked, and he didn't like that they immediately went to her job at Sweethearts. "We talk. We click. Y'all saw it that first night I went into Sweethearts. Hell, you teased me about it for days afterward."

Jacobe shrugged. "Yeah, because you don't typically go for the women we meet at places like that. I knew you were feeling her, but I didn't think you'd dump Bridget for her." He picked up his brush and ran it over the top of his low-cut fade. "That's some serious shit right there."

"None of you liked Bridget. I barely saw her over the past year. You can't tell me you think I'm crazy for splitting from her."

A chorus of *no*'s came from his friends. Will dropped his foot and pointed at Isaiah. "Bridget wasn't right for you, but that doesn't mean Angela is. You're ready to get married and have a bunch of babies. You really want to make her your wife?"

He did. The idea scared the mess out of him. That was one admission he wasn't ready to lay out to the world. "I'm with her. The end. We'll see where the future takes us."

Kevin chuckled. "Play on, playa. Enjoy your time with

ol' girl. She is fine. Just don't start spending all your money on her until you know she's legit."

Isaiah shook his head. "I don't know why y'all are talking to me as if I'm stupid. I know to wait and take my time before trusting any woman we meet."

The door to the locker room flew open and the three of them stood up. No one slammed into the locker room unless they were ready for trouble. Coach Gray stomped in and all of their shoulders relaxed. He glared at Isaiah.

Isaiah looked to his friends, then back at coach. "What?"

"You care to tell me why I just got a call from the local news station asking for a quote on my players screwing dancers in strip clubs?" he asked in a hard voice.

"The hell?" Isaiah demanded. Every eye turned on him.

"Yes," Coach Gray said. "They're doing an exposé. Apparently they've got recordings of you and some woman at Sweethearts. Come on, Isaiah, you're the good guy on the team. What the hell were you thinking? Right before the season starts, too." He ran his fingers through his thick brown hair and gritted his teeth.

Isaiah closed his eyes and cursed. Not good. This is why he typically considered the consequences of his actions. But Angela made him forget everything.

"Yo, Isaiah, you slept with this woman *at* Sweethearts?" Jacobe asked incredulously.

"I don't believe that," said Kevin.

"That's what I'm talking about!" Will laughed. "Isaiah, I didn't know you had it in you."

Isaiah opened his eyes and only looked at Coach. "It's not like that. We're dating. I didn't just go there and hook up with her."

"That only makes things marginally better." He

pointed at Isaiah. "Call your agent. Tell him before this goes live later this week. Get your story straight. Screwing your girlfriend at a strip club is better than screwing groupies. I'll handle things with the owners." He turned to walk away, then stopped and looked back. "And next time, take her to your place. Please." Coach left with a trail of curses and grumbles about the players giving him an early heart attack.

Kevin shook his head. "Sounds like you're about to be real serious about Angela."

Will chuckled. "At least until this story dies down."

Isaiah flipped them the bird. More out of frustration that his life was about to blow up in the media than anger at them. He pulled out his cell phone to call his agent. This was just the type of embarrassment and drama he'd tried to avoid. He didn't regret what happened with Angela, but a voice in his head that sounded a lot like his father questioned if feelings this wild and crazy, not to mention their unexpected consequences, were really good in the long term.

Chapter 19

When Angela told Isaiah she had to work that night, he'd offered to watch Cory. At first she'd considered saying no. She didn't want him to feel like she was using him for anything. Even something as small as babysitting. After the heads-up from Nate, though, she'd agreed. She needed to tell him about the news exposé and she preferred telling him to his face. After work, when she knew exactly how bad things were at the club with Z, was probably the best time to do it.

Her feet hurt and her body felt as heavy as lead when she finally put her key in the door to her apartment at 1:00 a.m. Thankfully she only had one more semester to work at Sweethearts. She was finally ready to admit the late nights working the bar weren't as easy as they'd been when she'd first started at the club. Her degree would hopefully lead to a promotion and the end of needing to work at Sweethearts.

The apartment was quiet, the lamp in the living room and the light from the television the only illumination as she entered. Kicking off the heels she'd been wearing, she hooked her fingers through the straps and carried them to the living area.

Cory slept on one end of the couch while Isaiah snored

softly on the other. An action movie from the eighties played on the television. Popcorn, pizza boxes, candy wrappers and soda cans littered the coffee table. Angela smiled and chuckled softly. Looked like they'd had a good time.

She put her shoes on a chair and tiptoed over to Isaiah first. His head leaned against the back of the couch and his legs were sprawled out in front of him. His lips were parted from his heavy breaths. He'd dressed casually to babysit, in a T-shirt and shorts, and looked so relaxed and cute she wanted to curl up in his lap and fall asleep in his arms. Instead, she gently shook his shoulder but resisted the urge to place a kiss on his cheek.

His eyes opened slowly, focused on her, and he smiled. "That's a sight worth waking up to," he said in a sexy, sleepy voice. He reached up and grabbed her waist, then tried to pull her into his lap.

Angela grinned and placed a hand on his chest. She nodded toward Cory. "I've got to get Cory in bed."

He squeezed her hip but let her go. Angela tapped Cory to wake him. He jerked awake and blinked several times, his gaze never quite focused.

"Come on, Cory. Time for bed," she said softly.

He nodded, mumbled something that sounded like *pizza*, then got up and shuffled to his room. A second later, his door closed. She glanced back at Isaiah. "Thanks again for watching him. You didn't have to."

"No problem at all. He's a good kid. Plus, he likes action movies and pizza. I can hang with him anytime."

Angela plopped down on the couch next to him. "Do you have to go right away?"

He lifted her feet and set them in his lap. "Does it look like I'm ready to leave?" He took one of her feet in his hands and massaged it.

Angela's head fell back and she groaned. "That feels... so good."

"I figured it would. You've been on your feet all night. In those shoes."

She lifted her gaze to him. He pointed to the heels she'd worn. "I don't usually wear heels, but I wanted to look extra nice today."

"Why?"

Might as well get to the bad news first. "So Z would maybe think twice about firing me."

Isaiah's hands slowed, but thankfully, he didn't stop massaging her foot. "Why would he fire you?"

Angela shifted until she was straighter on the couch but didn't pull her feet away. "A reporter is doing an exposé on local strip clubs. Apparently someone has—"

"A recording of a Gators player and the bartender," he said grimly, finishing her sentence.

Angela's jaw dropped. "You know? Why didn't you say something?"

"Because I wanted to talk to you face-to-face. Coach came to me earlier today. Why didn't you tell me?"

"Same reason. You don't bring up something like this over the phone." She pressed a hand to her temple. "This is terrible."

"Did Z fire you?"

She thought she heard a note of hopefulness in his voice, but his face revealed nothing. "No," she said forcefully. "I got an earful, and I won't be working any of the better shifts until the scrutiny dies down, but he doesn't want to let me go." She took a deep breath. "He's worried I'm getting played."

Isaiah switched to her other foot. "By me?"

"Yeah. When I told him we were dating, he looked skeptical. Z's had a lot of professional athletes come into his club and play around with the dancers. He said I shouldn't trust you."

Isaiah stilled and he met her gaze. "Do you?"

She wanted to. She really wanted to believe he was serious and not just having a little bit of fun. Expressing her doubts wouldn't make them go away. She'd just have to wait and see what he showed her. "I think you've been honest with me."

He chuckled and went back to the massage. "Not the same, but all right. I'll take that."

"So, what did your coach say?"

"That this is bad for the team. We don't need this type of publicity right before the season starts. That I'm the *good one* and he expected more of me."

Angela didn't know if expecting more meant don't have sex in a strip club or don't get caught having sex in a strip club. No need to ask, though. The coach's thoughts didn't matter. The only thing that mattered were Isaiah's feelings.

"What did you say to that?"

"I told him we're dating. I'm not fooling around being wild and crazy with women. When I gave my agent the heads-up, he said I should get ahead of the story."

"How?"

Isaiah soothed an extra sore spot on her foot and her eyes closed. "That feels fantastic," she moaned.

"Anything to make my woman happy. I'm hoping to make you moan in other ways in a minute." His expert hands slowed, traveled up her ankle and calf before he trailed his fingers down to her feet. The whisper of a caress caused a roar of sensation.

Angela squeezed her thighs together. "Finish your story before you start that."

His dark eyes blazed with desire and his grin was

wicked. "Okay. As far as getting ahead of the story, the team has an appearance tomorrow at Disney World. Part of the whole I'm-going-to-Disney thing after winning a championship. A lot of the players bring their wives and girlfriends. I'd like to bring you and Cory. We'll take pictures, answer a few reporter questions and the world will know you and I are dating. Then when the story hits, if our names are mentioned, the reports won't be about me sneaking in the back with a random bartender, but me sneaking off with my lady."

She wouldn't acknowledge how much him calling her his lady sparked pleasure in her heart. She forced her mind back to the other problem that would come from this story. "If they mention our names, then Mr. Cooper will know I work at Sweethearts."

He shrugged as if that was a minuscule thing. "You were already going to tell your supervisor that jerk Jerry saw you there."

"Seeing me is one thing. Finding out that you and I had sex in the back room via the local news is another." Worry hardened her tone. "I'll lose my job."

Her breathing sped up. She'd been so worried about Z, she hadn't spent a lot of time thinking ahead to Monday or the huge impact this story would potentially have on her main source of income.

"Shh." Isaiah reached over, placed his hand behind her head and pulled her forward. He kissed her gently. "Don't worry about that tonight. You can't do anything to change it. Tomorrow, email your supervisor and tell her you need to talk to her first thing. The sports reporters here are going with the team tomorrow and it'll hit the news that we're dating."

"Cory's spot in camp," Angela said. "I'll get him kicked out."

Isaiah brushed his hand over her cheek. "No, he won't. It's the last week of camp. I'll let Keri know this was all on me and I doubt she'll make Cory suffer because I fell for an angel."

He made everything sound so easy and reasonable. He had one thing right—there was little she could do about any of the problems at 1:00 a.m. on a Sunday morning. She leaned into his hand on her cheek and took a calming breath. "I'm glad you're optimistic. Optimism may not be enough to keep me employed."

"If it's not, I've got you."

She shook her head. "I don't need anyone to have me. I can take care of myself." She would not become dependent on him.

"Oh, really?" He clasped her waist, leaned back on the couch and pulled her on top of him.

Angela adjusted her legs until she straddled him. The hard press of his erection brushed against her sex and she gasped. "What are you doing?" Dumb question; she had more than an idea of what he was about.

"Taking care of you." He lifted a hand to the back of her head and pulled her down for a kiss. "One problem at a time. We'll do damage control. The story won't be as bad, and you won't lose your job."

She wanted to argue. To tell him his ability to give her amazing orgasms wasn't the same thing as taking care of her, but then his mouth bewitched her. Warmth spread over her as his hands roamed up her thighs until her short skirt bunched around her waist. Angela's hand dived beneath his shirt to play along the tight muscles of his stomach and chest. He gripped her ass and lifted his hips into the pocket of her thighs.

She let him take care of her, pushed aside everything that didn't matter this late at night. The only thing that did matter was this moment. His lips on her breasts after he tugged down the front of her tank top. His strong hands gently caressing across the skin of her thighs. Their suppressed moans and silent sighs as their passion grew. And when he covered himself, slid her underwear to the side and filled her completely, she didn't care about tomorrow, Monday, or any other day.

She bit into his shoulder to keep from screaming when the orgasm tore through her body. Isaiah's body jerked hard and deep within her with his own release. They remained in each other's embrace, one of his hands beneath her shirt on her back, the other running over her hair. He'd only pulled his pants down enough to slide into her and the front of his shirt was damp where her cheek lay pressed against his chest. Her sweat or his—who knew? Probably both.

"I know you're worried, and that you can take care of yourself," he said softly, his lips brushing against her forehead. "Just know that we're in this together. I won't leave you high and dry. I promise."

Angela's hands tightened their hold on his shirt. She didn't want to do this alone. She'd done so much on her own for so long. She didn't want Isaiah to be another person to disappoint her. "You say that now?" Her voice carried the teasing note she wanted to convey and not a hint of the fear trembling inside. Fear that she'd be left to clean up another mess in her life.

He lifted her chin and met her eye. Not a hint of teasing in his clear eyes. "I promise." Then he kissed her softly. Maybe it was the kiss, or the truth of his gaze, but she believed him, and that scared her more than him leaving.

Chapter 20

They fired her.

Angela sat in her car outside of the advocacy center. Her hands were clenched on the wheel, the box of personal items from her office on the passenger seat. She didn't bother to breathe in the lavender scent from her diffuser charm. There wasn't enough lavender in the world to settle her anger.

They'd made their new relationship official on Sunday. The media had eaten it up like a free all you can eat buffet. She'd given her supervisor the heads-up on Monday. The story had aired Wednesday. They waited until the end of the day on Friday to fire her.

"We don't need that type of publicity," Mr. Cooper had said. "The integrity of our advocates is the most important thing. I'm sorry, but working at a strip club and… doing things in the back room doesn't equal integrity."

Angela had to fight the urge to toss her stapler at his judgmental face. For him to question her integrity when she'd worked hard for them for years was laughable. Out of everyone there, she had the best record of volunteers actually visiting their assigned children. She'd won advocate of the year from the city last year. All of that down the drain because of one incident.

Angela sighed and hit the steering wheel. Jerry had smiled smugly at her as she'd walked out. She couldn't prove it, but she'd bet money he was the one who'd told Mr. Cooper that Angel from the story and Angela in the office were the same person.

She turned on the car and drove to pick up Cory. At least basketball camp was over. Keri had even offered to let him volunteer and help with the younger summer camp kids in the last few weeks before school would start. With no more camp, school a few weeks away and him turning fourteen soon, Angela had accepted she'd have to trust him enough to stay home alone in the evenings.

Keri was behind the counter, looking frazzled when Angela arrived.

"Hey, Keri, what's up?"

Keri sighed and ran a hand through her hair. "Our assistant director quit today." Keri's disbelieving tone said the resignation hadn't been expected.

"Why?"

"She got a new job in Miami. I can't blame her, but it leaves us in a bind. She handled a lot of the programming and budget stuff."

"That could be a good thing. You might get promoted." Angela tried for a bright side.

Keri cringed. "No. If I'm being honest, I don't want the responsibility. I like what I'm doing just fine."

"I'm sorry she left unexpectedly. Maybe I can catch some of her luck. I got fired today," Angela said.

"Oh, no! What happened?"

"Some foolishness." If Keri didn't automatically tie her and Isaiah to the story that aired, then Angela wasn't going to make the leap for her. "No worries. I've got a part-time job I can get more hours from. I'll start looking for a new day job tomorrow."

Keri's eyes brightened. "Well, maybe you should consider our assistant-director position? I've worked with you over the years and I think you can handle it."

"Really? I've always veered toward social work."

"You'd be helping people here, plus, we need someone with some sense," Keri added with a laugh.

Cory came from the back then. "Maybe I'll think about it." Angela waved and walked over to Cory. She didn't look for Isaiah. He said he was leaving camp early for preseason stuff. She was glad he wasn't there. She was still processing that they'd fired her. She didn't want him to witness her in angry, freak-out mode. Once they were settled in the car, she told Cory about getting fired.

"Why?" he asked.

Thankfully, Cory hadn't seen the news report. And if he had, he hadn't mentioned it to her. Which was perfectly fine. "Office politics. Things are going to be tight for a while until I find another job."

"Are you going to postpone going to school?"

She shook her head. "Not if I can help it. This is my last semester. I really need to finish. If I have to take out a loan, I will."

"Why?" When Angela gave him a questioning look, Cory laughed. "You're dating a baller now, Auntie. Just ask Isaiah for the money." He said it as if the solution was obvious.

"No. I'm not with Isaiah because of his money. I'm not going to ask him to pay my bills."

"I'm sure he wouldn't mind. He really likes you. When a man likes a woman, he likes to take care of her."

Angela gripped the steering wheel. The boy was young and this was an opportunity to school him. "If a woman can take care of herself, then her man should respect her decisions and let her handle things on her own."

"If you say so. I just know he wouldn't want to see you struggling. If he wants to help out, I don't see the problem in letting him."

"When you're older and have gotten through tough times on your own, then you'll understand."

They went back to the apartment. A few teens were outside playing basketball at the complex's goal. Cory decided to go hang with them and Angela was glad to get a few minutes to decompress after her terrible day. She changed, then powered up her laptop to start the job search. The position Keri's boss vacated wasn't listed yet. She'd never considered working at a place like the activity center. If Keri thought it was a good fit, then it wouldn't hurt to apply. It wasn't like she had a backup plan for getting fired from the advocacy center.

She'd been on the computer for half an hour when someone knocked on the door. Assuming it was Nate, who'd agreed to sit with Cory while she worked tonight, she yelled for the person to come in.

"Do you always just let people in without checking?" It was Isaiah's voice.

The very sight of him improved her mood. He wore a pair of gray shorts and a white shirt that complemented his sleek build. She jumped out of the chair and walked over to kiss him. Strong arms wrapped around her. "What are you doing here? I thought you had team stuff."

"That was earlier. I'm free for the evening. I decided to come over and see you."

"I'm glad you decided to come over." She pulled him onto the couch.

His fingers ran over the back of her hand. "I saw Cory outside—he said you were fired today."

"The director doesn't believe I have enough integrity

to work as a child advocate." She tried not to sound bitter by mocking Mr. Cooper's holier-than-thou tone.

Her attempt to lighten the heaviness of their conversation didn't erase the concern on his face. "Why didn't you call me?"

"It happened right at the end of the day." Plus she hadn't wanted to call Isaiah and complain. This was her problem to solve.

"What are you going to do?"

She sighed. "I was just on the computer looking for jobs. Until I find something, I'll take on extra shifts at Sweethearts. Z asked me to hold back, but when he hears I was fired, he'll help out."

Isaiah's body tightened. "You don't need to work extra shifts."

"Yes, I do. How else am I going to pay the rent, let alone school?"

He took her hand in his. "I can help with—"

She shook her head before he even finished the sentence. They'd just started dating. She wasn't about to ask him to pay her bills. "No. I am not taking your money. I've been through worse. I can handle this."

"But I want to help."

"And I appreciate it. Look, if things get really bad then I'll let you know and maybe—" she lifted a finger "—just maybe you can help with something. But until then, let me at least try to get myself back on my feet."

He looked ready to argue, stilled, then relaxed and nodded. Apparently her wishes overruled the argument in his head. She appreciated him accepting her wishes instead of pushing the issue. She really liked Isaiah, would probably fall in love with him if things continued to go well and she knew she could trust him.

Angela leaned forward and kissed him. The kiss was

meant to be brief, but Isaiah pulled her onto his lap and deepened it. Heat swirled inside her.

"I've got to go to work," she said against his lips.

He groaned and gripped her thighs. "You're working tonight? I thought we could hang out."

She'd rather stay here with him, but she really couldn't afford to skip out of work. "I know, but I really need to go now that it's my only source of income."

"What about Cory?"

"Nate is watching him."

"Look, save your teen-sitter money," he said with a grin. "At least let me do this for you. Cory can spend the night at my place."

"Why spend the night?"

He leaned forward and whispered in her ear. "Because if he stays, you stay." His hand slid up her thigh until his fingers brushed the heat of her center. "And I miss you."

Angela sighed and kissed him harder. She should save the money. *Yeah, that's why you're going to agree.* "I'll be there before one."

Chapter 21

Isaiah had just left a team meeting about the upcoming training camp when his mother called. He had been sitting with several members of the team in the locker room talking and stepped out to answer.

"Bridget told me you dumped her for some stripper" were the first words out of her mouth.

Isaiah gritted his teeth to keep from snapping at his mother. He didn't mind her asking about what had happened with Bridget, but the derisive way she'd said "stripper" set him on edge. She'd already formed an opinion about Angela before she'd even met her. He had no doubt Bridget helped with that.

"Hello to you, too," he said calmly.

"Isaiah, I didn't call you to play games," she answered in an equally calm tone, the one she used when she was mad but tried to use reason to get her way. "What's going on?"

"For one, I didn't dump Bridget. She wanted time to figure out if we should get back together. I told her about Angela and that I didn't think getting back together was a good idea."

"Why did you invite Bridget to move there if you were interested in another woman?" Her voice was measured and questioning. She sounded every bit the college professor asking a pupil to dig deeper to find the true answer to the equation.

"I hadn't met Angela when I first suggested moving to Bridget," he answered just as evenly.

"Aha," she said slowly. "You're making a rash decision."

Isaiah inhaled and exhaled slowly. "You'd rather I continue to keep Bridget in my life while I date Angela?"

"No, but you basically told Bridget you two were done forever after only knowing this woman briefly. You and Bridget have known each other for years. You've got a lot in common and want the same things."

"We only came back to each other because it was convenient, not because we cared for each other. I don't love her."

She was quiet for a few seconds. "Who is this woman?" The change in subject meant he'd won the argument as it related to Bridget. His mother may have an engineer's mind, but she also believed in love. "And why did you introduce her to the media before us?"

"Introducing her to the media first wasn't intentional." Calculated to prevent fallout, but not to disregard his family.

"You're showing her off for damage control," she said as if she'd caught him cheating on a final exam. "Your father heard about the incident."

Of course his father knew. "We were together before the appearance."

"Not for long. You'd just split with Bridget a few days earlier."

His mother never questioned him this hard about the women he'd occasionally been seen with when he wasn't with Bridget. He was sure they would have been happy with whomever he ultimately fell in love with even if the woman wasn't Bridget. This was something different.

"What are you getting at?" he asked.

"We're coming to see you before you leave for training camp. We want to meet her," she said in a no-nonsense voice that meant the bags were packed and plane tickets purchased.

"Mom—"

"Obviously you went through a lot of trouble to clean things up where this woman—"

"Angela."

"Where *Angela* is concerned. For years, you've never walked away from Bridget for any other pretty face that's crossed your path. Nor have you introduced a woman to the media. If you're going to be serious about her, then we want to meet her."

"And you'll do a background check on her before you come." He was only half-teasing.

"No. We'll let you reveal all her dirty secrets to us in person," his mom said sweetly.

They talked for a few more minutes before saying goodbye. He swore under his breath before going back into the locker room for his stuff. Mark Simmons, one of his teammates who'd been drafted the previous year, stopped him. Isaiah concealed his frustration. He had no problems with Mark, but they weren't close. Mark was brash, cocky and liked flaunting the money, women and privilege that came with being a professional athlete.

"Isaiah, I saw your girl at Sweethearts last night." Mark licked his lips. "She's pretty fine. I might get her to serve me every time I go." Mark giggled as if he'd just said something funny.

"What did you just say?" Isaiah glared and stepped to Mark.

Mark's eyes widened but he didn't back down. "I know you ain't rolling up on me over that chick."

Isaiah pointed in Mark's face. "That's my girl, not some chick. Don't talk about her like that."

"Don't get mad at me because she's one of the packages there. Me and a hundred other fellas are checking out all her assets every night."

Isaiah lunged forward, but Kevin held him back. "Hold up. Not in here. This ain't worth it."

Mark shook his head. "Listen to your boy." He walked out.

Isaiah shook off Kevin's arm. "I'm good."

"You sure, man?"

"Yes. He needs to watch his mouth."

Kevin stepped forward. "And you need to fix your reaction," he said in a low voice so the other players in the locker room couldn't hear. "Angela is cool, but she does work in a strip club. Mark won't be the only guy trying to get under your skin with that. If you're going to be with her, then you gotta accept that."

Kevin hit his shoulder, then gave him a look that said, "You good?" Isaiah nodded, but he wasn't good. He grabbed his stuff and left the arena. Kevin was right. Hell, opponents would try to use Angela to get under his skin. It happened all the time. Just last season Jacobe had almost missed the playoffs because of a personal jab on the court. As long as she worked there, his relationship with her was an open target.

Chapter 22

Cory practically skipped next to Angela as she walked into the main office of her apartment complex to pay the rent. Despite getting fired, she focused on the good and kept a bounce to her step. She'd find another job, Cory hadn't had a teenage meltdown in weeks and things were going really well with her and Isaiah. Life could be a lot worse.

"Are you sad Isaiah has to leave for training camp?" Cory asked.

She glanced at him with a smile. "I'm going to miss him, but I'm not sad. It's a part of his job." Even though it was a Saturday and she would have raked in on tips that were desperately needed, she'd asked Z to let her have the night off since Isaiah would leave for training at the end of the week. She didn't want to spend his last weekend in town serving drinks to strangers.

"I'm surprised you didn't ask me to hang with Nate tonight." Cory opened the door to the office for her.

"You'll miss him as much as I do, plus, he wanted both of us to come over for dinner," she said. The cool air of the office was welcome after the heat outside. "You two will probably ignore me while you play video games half the night anyway."

Cory laughed and followed her inside. "Yeah, that sounds about right."

Not that she cared. Cory would pass out from video-game overload and then she and Isaiah would have plenty of alone time. Her lips lifted in a smile and her body shivered in anticipation.

She walked over to the drop box for the checks and pulled the envelope with next month's rent out of her purse. Thankfully, she had some savings and wouldn't struggle too hard over the upcoming month. School started for her and Cory when Isaiah got back. Not working would free up time for her to study during the day while Cory was at school.

Sheila, the weekend property manager, came out of the office and grinned. "Hey, Angela, what are you doing here?"

Angela held up her envelope. "Paying the rent for next month."

Sheila's eyebrows drew together. "Why?"

"So I'll have a place to stay for another thirty days?"

"Don't be silly," Sheila said with a hand wave. "Your rent is covered for the next six months."

Angela cocked her head to the side. "What are you talking about?"

Sheila's eyes widened. "I thought you knew. He didn't say it was a surprise."

"Who didn't say it was a surprise?" Angela asked sharply.

"Your boyfriend, Isaiah Reynolds. He stopped by earlier this week and covered your rent. There's only six months left on your lease, so that's what he covered. I do hope you'll consider renewing with us after that time."

Angela crushed the envelope in her hand. He'd paid her rent. Without consulting her or saying anything. She'd asked him to wait and let her try to figure things out first. Why hadn't he? Did he think she couldn't handle herself? Did he think she'd want him to spend money on her like this? Was that what he thought their relationship was about?

She wouldn't become dependent on him. She wouldn't become dependent on anyone. Depending on someone increased the risk of struggling even harder when they left her high and dry. She wasn't going through that again.

"Thank you for telling me. I didn't know." She looked at Cory. "Come on, let's go."

Cory didn't say anything as he followed her out of the office. Once they were in the car he gave her a wary glance. "What's wrong? I thought you'd be happy about having the rent paid."

Angela used the time it took to back out of the parking space to take a deep breath and get her frustration under control. When they were out of the complex she spoke. "I appreciate his effort, but he shouldn't have done that without talking to me first."

"Maybe he wanted to surprise you. There's nothing wrong with surprising you, is there?" Cory sounded genuinely confused.

"We'd already talked and I told him I didn't want him to step in. I have things under control. For him to step in and take over like that after I asked him not to means he doesn't respect my wishes."

Cory plucked at a string on the edge of his gray khaki shorts. "Or he just really likes you and wants to help. Like when you tell me to eat my vegetables because they're good for me."

"Not the same."

"Sounds the same." Cory's phone chimed and he got sucked into a text conversation.

Angela welcomed the interruption. She didn't know how to explain the dynamics of relationships to Cory. He'd seen her look for a job every day. They'd make it through the upcoming month and then the next. The third month would be hard. She couldn't lie; not having to worry about rent would be a relief, but that didn't mean Isaiah could just step in and handle her life.

Cory focused on his phone for the remainder of the time it took to get to Isaiah's place. There were two cars there besides his that she didn't recognize. Maybe a few of his teammates, which meant she'd have to save the discussion about him overstepping his bounds until later.

They got out of the car and rang the bell. Isaiah answered the door. His face brightened the second he saw her. Her heart fluttered and tightened. Damn, she was crazy about him.

"Right on time," Isaiah said. "Come on in."

He gave Cory a shoulder-bump hug. When he pulled her into his arms for a hug and then kissed her neck, her body hummed. She was really crazy about him.

You're mad at him, too.

She stiffened and pulled back. Isaiah frowned but since Cory watched them she didn't want to get into the argument now.

"I saw cars out front," she said quickly. "Do you have friends over?"

His smile was a little tight. "Not really. Come on in." He took her hand and led her and Cory farther inside. "My family is here."

Angela stopped walking. Her heart froze, then rushed to catch up with her whirling thoughts. "Your family?" she asked tightly. She tugged on her plain navy maxi dress and smoothed her hair. "You didn't tell me they would be here."

"Surprise?" he said with a half grin. He tugged on her hand. "Come on, it won't be bad. They came to town to see me before training camp."

"I could have come later, or another day."

"I want them to meet you. And they want to meet you, too." She must have made a look because concern filled his gaze and he stepped closer. "It's not a big deal. They're in town, I want to spend time with you before I go, that's all. Don't panic."

"I'm not panicking." Her voice sounded calm. Her palms were sweaty. Maybe she was slightly panicked. "I'm just caught off guard."

"Don't worry." He squeezed her hand reassuringly. "They'll love you just as much as I do."

Angela couldn't breathe again. He loved her? Did he mean that the way she thought he did, or was he just reassuring her? How did she feel if it was the first way? He must have taken her stunned silence as her being okay with moving forward, because he nodded to Cory and took them outside to the patio.

The small amount of time it took to get to the patio out back wasn't enough to let her brain register everything that was happening. He'd paid her rent, was introducing her to his parents and kinda said he loved her. Everything was too much, too soon. She needed time to process. She liked the idea of where their relationship seemed to be going, but not this quickly. If she wasn't careful she'd cave to the urge to dive headfirst into this and he'd snatch everything away just as quickly. She'd be left with nothing but fond memories and the confirmation she could only rely on herself again.

His entire family really had come into town. Four people sat around a glass table, sipping lemonade and soaking up the sunshine. The smell of charcoal from a grill nearby filled the air. His parents were easy to pick out. The handsome older couple suited each other. His dad was just as tall as Isaiah, with the same pecan-brown complexion and expressive eyes. He looked relaxed in a pair of dark slacks and a polo shirt. His mom gave Angela a friendly, if not guarded, smile. Her salt-and-pepper hair was cut short to complement her heart-shaped face, and the peach-colored sundress draped her curvy figure and enhanced her dark skin.

His mother came over to Angela and clasped one of her hands. "Angela, it's so great to finally meet you. We've heard so much about you." He voice was warm, her shoulders relaxed, but her eyes were sharp as they watched Angela closely.

Exactly whom had she heard so much about Angela from? "It's nice to meet you, too, Mrs. Reynolds. This is my nephew, Cory."

"Call me Linda," she said before releasing her hand and smiling at Cory. "Such a tall boy. How old are you?"

"Almost fourteen," Cory said with teenage pride.

Linda laughed. "I remember when my boys were that age. They ate me out of house and home."

"That's the same thing Auntie always says," Cory said with a smile.

Linda nodded and focused back on Angela. "He lives with you?"

"Yes."

Linda waited, but Angela offered no other explanation.

Linda nodded slightly and one eyebrow quirked just a fraction. "Isaiah, introduce your lady to the rest of the family."

Isaiah's father was nice and watched her with the same underlying skepticism she'd sensed in Linda. His brother, Tim, resembled Isaiah without an athlete's build and was a few inches shorter. His fiancée, April, a stylish woman who eyed Angela with obvious curiosity in her light brown gaze, greeted her next.

Isaiah and Angela settled on one of the outdoor sofas. Cory asked Isaiah if he could play a video game upstairs in the media room, but Linda said there was no reason for him to run off and suggested they all get to know each other.

Cory opted to help the men work the grill. Linda and April chatted with Angela. "We already made a salad and coleslaw for later," Linda said. "We'll let the men handle the burning of the meat."

The conversation flowed easily and stayed away from anything sensitive. After about thirty minutes, Angela felt more relaxed. Though Linda watched her closely, she didn't pry or make Angela feel uncomfortable. After they ate and talked a little more, Angela had almost forgotten she was mad at Isaiah.

She went inside to get more ice and Isaiah followed her in. He walked up behind her at the fridge and wrapped his arms around her waist. "Is it bad that I can't wait for my family to get the hell out of the house so we can have some time together?"

Angela chuckled and leaned back into the strength of his embrace. "Cory will still be here."

"Yes, but Cory is easily distracted by video games." He kissed the side of her neck, then inhaled deeply. "You smell delicious."

Angela turned in his arms and hugged his waist. She made sure to keep her glass with the ice in it off his back. "Then you'll have to taste me later."

He groaned and kissed her hard. When they came up for air he didn't let her go. "I think my family likes you."

"You're lucky your family is here. I was angry at you when I came over."

His eyebrows drew together and he pulled back. "Why?"

She pulled out of his embrace. Mustering indignation was hard when she was in his arms. "You paid my rent for six months. Why did you do that?"

He shrugged as if that was no big deal. "I didn't want you to worry while you got your finances in order."

His nonchalance turned up her anger real quick. "I'm not worried. I have a handle on things."

"Why are you upset? That's one less thing to worry about during your last semester." He rubbed the back of his neck. "You won't have to work so many hours at the club."

Her suspicions peaked. "Working those extra hours is the reason I have things under control. I don't need to be rescued."

"Well, I don't need my woman working harder than she has to when I can step in and make things easier."

"That's not the point. You went against my wishes."

"I did something nice for you. I can't believe you're giving me grief over this. I'd think you'd be happy to not have guys drooling down your cleavage during your last semester of school."

Angela took a step back. "That's what this is really about? Guys drooling down my cleavage?"

He crossed his arms. "I wouldn't be heartbroken if you didn't work there."

The realization was like a slap to the face. "Why is this suddenly a problem? Is this because of the thing with Jerry, or the news investigation?"

"It's because you don't have to be there anymore.

You're with me. I can handle things until you're back on your feet." He reached for her hands.

Angela pulled her hands back. "No, this isn't just about that. You weren't upset about me working there when we met. What changed?"

"What changed is that we're together now. You're my woman, how does it look for me to let you hang out behind a bar in a strip club with half the men in the area, and on my team, drooling over you and telling me about it the next day."

Angela sucked in a breath. "You're worried about what other people are going to think? Are you embarrassed by my job?"

"I'm not embarrassed, but that doesn't mean I have to like it. I can get you out of there."

Angela held up a finger. "News flash! You don't have to get me out of anywhere."

The door to the patio opened. Cory walked in with Isaiah's brother, Tim. Their smiles died when they heard the last of Angela's angry statement. They looked from her to Isaiah curiously. Angela couldn't stay another minute. She'd end up saying something she would regret.

"Cory, grab your stuff. We're going," she said.

Cory sucked his teeth. "But, Auntie, I was just about to get on the game."

"I don't care, it's time to go."

Isaiah stepped forward. "Angela, let's talk. Don't leave like this."

She met his gaze. "Are you saying you're sorry for paying my rent without telling me and that you're willing to talk to me before stepping in and taking over my finances?"

Isaiah rubbed the bridge of his nose. "I was only trying to help."

"And I'm only telling you that I'm not looking for a dictator."

Chapter 23

"You know her leaving is for the best."

Tim's voice interrupted Isaiah's vain attempt to watch television in his upstairs media room. Isaiah leaned back in the chair and pinched the bridge of his nose.

"Did you pick the small straw or something?" Isaiah asked, feeling weary. After Angela left, he'd gone upstairs to get away from his family's prying eyes and questioning probes.

Tim came into the room and sank onto the couch next to Isaiah. "I'm the one you're most likely to listen to. That was the way it was when you were in high school and that hasn't changed."

"This isn't like high school," Isaiah said.

"Isn't it? You fall for the wrong girl, try to help her out and things turn out badly. You still haven't learned your lesson."

"I'm not doing anything wrong being with Angela, or trying to help her."

"Maybe not, but you still can't help yourself when you see a damn damsel in distress," Tim said with a chuckle. "You trying to help Angela is no different than when you chained yourself to a fence to stop the university from tearing down the project homes Veronica stayed in. You were so in love and ready to save her you didn't stop to think about the consequences. You lost a scholarship and nearly cost Mom her job at the university."

"It wasn't that bad."

"It wasn't that good, either. Think of what it'll mean to be with Angela. You're the good guy of the league. You don't need a woman you'll have to defend all the time."

"Who says I'll have to defend her? I care about her. This isn't a teenage crush and I'm not jumping into something because my hormones told me to do it." He was tired of being judged because of one bad decision when he was much younger.

"Are you sure? The incident at the club? You broke up with Bridget after being with her for years. I'm not sure you're really thinking with the head on your shoulders versus the head below your belt. Make sure you know what you're doing before you go after her. Bridget is still interested. She cares about you. Don't let go of a woman who's doing something and going somewhere, because of a pretty face and a tight body."

Isaiah glared at his brother. "She's more than a pretty face. And she's going somewhere. Angela worked as an advocate for kids in the foster system before the incident at the club cost her the job. She's also a damn good bartender and using the money she makes at the club to finish graduate school. Just because she isn't a lawyer, doesn't mean she's a lesser person."

He didn't regret paying her rent. He would do it again if it made things easier on her, but listening to Tim malign her position made him realize he shouldn't have made a big deal about her quitting. She was a lot more than her job. He was just as wrong by diminishing her to just that.

Isaiah stood abruptly. "I've got to go." He hurried toward the door.

"Isaiah, are you sure?" Tim called after him.

"Yes, I'm sure." He walked out and nearly ran into his mother on the other side of the door. She wore the look in her face that she had when she'd picked him up at the police station for chaining himself to a fence for love. "Mom, don't try to stop me."

She held up a hand. "I'm not. I like Angela. She's a smart woman and she likes you."

"Then you know I have to go after her and apologize?"

"I just want you to be happy. And to be sure. It's unfair to her and Bridget if you change your mind later."

Isaiah nodded. "Bridget isn't the woman I fell in love with."

Chapter 24

Angela shoved the key into the door of her apartment. "Cory, for the last time, I'm not talking about Isaiah." She pointed at him and glared when his mouth formed the start of a *but*. "No *buts*. I'm done." She pushed open the door and entered the apartment. "I'll order a pizza and we can watch a movie or something. We can have our own fun."

Cory huffed but didn't say anything else. He'd asked a million times in the car why she fought with Isaiah and why they'd left. He'd thought it was the money, and while she was still annoyed about that she wasn't about to explain that besides the money, Isaiah had a problem with her serving drinks at a strip club. He'd met her there, for goodness sake!

This was why she didn't date men she met at the club. They always got a chip on their shoulder eventually and thought their manhood would be in question because of her job. She'd hoped Isaiah would be different. It hurt that he wasn't.

Her home phone rang soon after she and Cory were settled on the couch to pick a movie, him still sullen about leaving and her still aggravated.

She answered and the familiar recording that told

her she had a collect call from the jail made her stiffen. Her brother. He didn't call much, and hadn't called since Heather hightailed it to New York.

"It's your dad," Angela said before accepting the call. Cory perked up on his side of the couch. He faced her with an eager look on his young face.

"Hey, Angela, how's it going?" Darryl's deep voice said without a trace of true interest in her well-being.

"Darryl, what's up? Are you okay?" She wished she could act indifferent, the way he could, but her concern seeped through. He was the only family she had left besides her aunt, whom she didn't really consider family anymore. Even though he'd done something stupid and left her and Cory in a lurch, she couldn't stop caring about her brother.

"Yeah, everything is good. Just calling to check in."

She relaxed just a little and smiled at her nephew. "Cory is here. Want to talk to him?"

Cory's eager expression turned into a happy grin and he held out his hand to take the phone.

"Nah. Not today," Darryl said quickly.

Angela frowned. Cory read her expression and his hand dropped. "Really?" she asked. "When was the last time you spoke to him?"

"Look I only have a few minutes. I can't spend a lot of time listening to him talk about girls and stuff." Darryl's voice rose and agitation filled his tone.

She didn't give a damn about his time. What small amount of time he got should be spent telling his son he was sorry for screwing everything up. "I can't believe you," Angela snapped. "He's right here."

Cory jumped up and ran down the hall. His door slammed a second later. "He was here. You hurt his feelings. Seriously, Darryl, I've tried to be on your side.

When you went to jail, I didn't want to think you were a terrible father but to refuse to talk to Cory? Damn, why did you call?"

"I called because Heather isn't answering my calls. I think she's laid up with a man."

Angela rolled her eyes. "News flash, the judge broke you two up."

"Save that bull. She's also talking about not coming back. What do you have to say about that?"

Angela's world tilted. She leaned forward and placed her forehead in her hand. "What? Are you sure?"

"That's why I'm calling. Have you talked to her?"

Angela thought about the last time she'd heard from Heather. "Not since she dropped off Cory. She said she would be back."

"Well, you better check. I think she's done with us."

"I'll call her now." There wasn't anything else to say to Darryl. They ended the call and Angela immediately called Heather's number. She didn't get an answer so she gripped the phone and waited for the voice message.

"Heather, this is Angela. I need you to call me immediately. I spoke with Darryl. He said you're planning to stay in New York permanently. What about Cory? You can't just leave him behind like this. Call me."

She ended the call and cursed. Cory didn't deserve any of this. What could possibly possess Heather to forget about her child and stay in New York? Angela really hadn't expected her to return before the start of school, but she had thought that before they really got into the year, Heather would return or at least send for Cory.

Cory's door cracked open. His dark eyes looked out at her. "Mom's not coming back?"

Angela really wished she could have five minutes

alone in a room with Heather for the wounded look in Cory's eyes. "I don't know, Cory. I'm trying to reach her."

"What happens if you don't reach her?"

Angela took a deep breath. She didn't know the answer. Heather disappearing didn't automatically put Cory in her custody. They'd have to go through the system to provide Angela with any legal rights, but would Darryl or Heather really sign off on that? The entire situation was complicated.

Someone knocked on the door. Angela glanced from Cory to the front door. "I don't know," she said before going to answer it.

Isaiah stood on the other side. At once she was happy and angry. She wrestled with the urge to jump into his arms for comfort and slam the door in his hypocritical face.

His eyebrows drew together and he stepped closer to the entrance. "What happened? Are you okay?"

His concern pushed her closer to the jump-in-his-arms side of the debate. Before she could do anything she had to know why he'd come. "What are you doing here?"

"I won't accept that we're done before we even had the chance to get started," he said. "I'm falling in love with you, Angela, and because of that, I won't let one disagreement be the end of us. If you feel even a little bit of the same for me, then I know you don't want this to end, either." He put his palm against the door and pushed it farther open. He didn't come in, just stood close enough for her to smell his cologne as he stared into her eyes. "Do you feel the same?"

She couldn't say no. Not when her heart raced and tendrils of happiness as strong as steel wormed their way into her heart. He was falling in love with her. He hadn't just been talking earlier. If he loved her, and he'd come here to apologize, maybe they could make this work.

"I feel the same," she said softly.

A huge smile broke out on his face. He swept her into his arms and kissed her. She allowed herself the moment to be happy. To bask in the pleasure of knowing things with Isaiah would be okay.

He kicked her door closed and carried her into the apartment, his strong arms around her waist and hers around his shoulders.

"I'm glad someone's happy." Cory's angry voice interrupted their moment.

Angela pushed on Isaiah's chest and he let her go. Guilt for her moment of joy when Cory's world had crumbled rose up. "Cory, being happy about one thing doesn't mean I don't care about your problem."

Isaiah stood behind her with a hand on her shoulder. He pulled her back against his chest. "What problem?"

Cory crossed his arms. His lips pressed into a tight line and he looked away. Angela glanced back at Isaiah. "My brother called. Heather—Cory's mother—told him she's not coming back, and that she's not sending for Cory. I tried to call her, but she didn't answer."

"What are you going to do?"

Angela shrugged. "I don't know. There are a lot of things that'll need to be worked out."

"I'm not a problem to be solved," Cory said angrily.

Angela went back to him and placed a hand on his arm. "I'm not saying you are."

Cory jerked away. "I don't need your pity." He spun away and stomped back to his room.

Angela took a few steps after him, but Isaiah stopped her with a hand on her elbow. "Give him a few minutes to calm down. Tell me what else happened and then I can try to talk to him."

She looked at Cory's door, then nodded. "Nothing else to tell. On top of that my brother didn't even want to talk to him on the phone."

"What?" Anger flared in Isaiah's eyes. He threw a look at Cory's door. "I'll stick around tonight and we'll somehow convince him everything will be okay. We won't leave him high and dry."

Angela nodded and Isaiah pulled her into the comfort of his arms. There was so much more they needed to talk about, but she and Isaiah's problems could wait. Tonight, they needed to make sure Cory understood he wasn't alone.

Chapter 25

The sound of something crunching woke Isaiah the following morning. He jerked up and a sharp pain shot down his back. He groaned and rested his head back. He was on the couch in Angela's living room. The last thing he remembered the night before was resting his head in Angela's lap while they watched a movie. They'd finally convinced Cory to come out of his room and hang with them, but only after he made them promise not to talk about his mom or dad. They'd agreed, feeling Cory needed time to process. There was a blanket over him, which meant he must have fallen asleep and Angela left him where he was.

Stifling a groan, Isaiah turned his head in the direction of the crunching sound. Cory sat on the chair next to the couch eating cereal from a bowl. He lifted his chin in a what's-up motion and shoveled another spoonful of cereal into his mouth.

Isaiah eased into a sitting position and tried to massage the kink out of his neck. "Could you chew any louder?"

Cory half chuckled. "I thought you'd be sleeping in Auntie's room since you made up."

He'd thought so, too. Her bed was much preferable to the short couch. "I don't mind the couch." He rolled his neck to loosen the knots. He leaned his forearms on his legs and really took in Cory. "How are you doing?"

Cory shrugged. "All right, I guess."

"You guess? Remember what I told you. You can talk to me. What's going on in your head?"

Cory broke eye contact to stare at the cereal in his bowl. "I'm mad…at my dad and my mom."

"I can understand that."

"They don't miss me at all," Cory continued. "The only person who ever misses me is Denise."

"Denise? The girl from camp?" He'd expected Cory to say Angela.

Cory nodded. "It's like she's the only one who cares, but it shouldn't be like that. My mom and dad should care."

Isaiah slid over on the couch and gently bumped Cory's knee with his hand. Cory looked up and Isaiah met his eyes. "She's not the only one who cares. I care. Your aunt cares. You understand that, don't you?"

"I guess," he mumbled.

"No guessing. Know it. We'll figure this out, but regardless of what happens, we both have your back. Got that?"

Cory nodded and he looked a little more convinced than he had a second ago. Angela's bedroom door opened and she stepped out. Her hair was pulled back into a loose knot and she wore a pair of turquoise pajama pants with a white T-shirt. The pajamas weren't sexy in the typical sense of the word, but that didn't stop thoughts of cuddling with her in a comfortable bed and all her soft curves against him from popping into Isaiah's head. He wanted to jump up, cross the room and pull her into his arms.

"Good morning," she said as she walked into the room.

"I heard you two talking and figured I'd better get up and make breakfast."

She stopped at Cory's chair, placed her hand on his shoulder and leaned down to kiss the top of his head. Cory twisted away, but he had a smile on his face. "I got breakfast."

"I see that," she said. She met Isaiah's gaze. "Want anything more substantial than cereal?"

"I do, but you don't have to cook. Why don't we go out for breakfast? Then we can get back to my place and have lunch with my family before they leave later today."

Angela bit her lower lip. "Breakfast is fine, but I can't do lunch. I've got to get back here and finish registering for school before going in to work tonight."

Isaiah's body stiffened. "Work?"

She must have heard the tightness in his voice because she crossed her arms. "Yes. Work."

"Do you really think you should be working tonight?" He looked pointedly at Cory, who was once again focused on eating cereal.

"What else should I be doing? I'm the one who has to keep the roof over our heads."

"In case you forgot, for the next six months your roof is paid for."

"That's not my only bill. My first payment to the school is due at the end of the week."

Unease swept through Isaiah. His next words were going to piss her off. "That's covered, too."

Her jaw dropped and her arms uncrossed to fall at her sides. Cory looked between the two of them, stood and went into the kitchen. Smart kid to avoid the shots about to be fired.

"You paid my tuition?"

"I told you I would help."

"I was willing to forgive the rent, but this. What the hell, Isaiah? Are you trying to make me dependent on you?"

He shot to his feet. "Of course not."

"Because you've got another think coming if you think I'll let you turn me into one of those women completely dependent on her man. You won't control my life only to drop me later with no way to support myself once you move on."

He held up a hand and tried to process her accusations. "Move on? I just told you I'm falling in love with you. Who the hell says I'm moving on?"

"Love is respecting my wishes. Not going behind my back."

He pinched the bridge of his nose. "We're having the same damn fight we had yesterday. I thought we were going to make this work."

"Only if you admit that what you did was wrong."

"I won't because it wasn't. My woman needed my help and I gave it to her."

"See, there you go again. *Your woman*, as if I'm some pet you have to take care of. I've been blindsided before. Not again." She stomped across the room to her purse and pulled out her checkbook. "How much do I owe you?"

"Don't be silly. You can't afford to pay me back."

She turned and threw the checkbook at him. It hit him in the chest and fell to the floor. "Damn you, Isaiah! I won't let you control my life."

His own anger spiked. Isaiah glared at the ceiling and gritted his teeth to keep from screaming in frustration. When he looked back at her his body was rigid. "I don't understand where this is coming from. You want me to apologize for paying your bills? Fine, I apologize, but I'm not going to sit by and do nothing. Things are about to get hard with Cory. Quit working at that club and let me help out."

"We're back to that now? That's what this was all about?" Her voice dripped with accusation. "Tell me you care, show me all the things you're doing for me, tell me what I'm going to do."

"Will you stop being paranoid and trying to turn this into some plot to control you."

She pointed to the door. "Get out."

"What?"

"I want you out of my face before I throw something harder than a checkbook at you."

Isaiah's frustration snapped. His neck hurt, he was tired and he needed to leave before he said something equally ridiculous. "I'm gone."

"Good."

He glared at her, but she raised her chin defiantly. Shaking his head, he snatched up his keys and stalked out. He stood with his back to her door for a second, angry, frustrated and confused. What the hell just happened? Her dead bolt snapped into place. Was it even worth it to try and make things work with someone so stubborn?

Chapter 26

"You have got to be the craziest woman in the state of Florida," Vicki said, shaking her head and looking at Angela as if she wanted to drive her to the nearest mental facility.

Angela crossed her arms. "I can't believe you don't see my side in this."

The music in the club didn't block Vicki's snort of disbelief. Sapphire hurried over and waved her hands impatiently. "You got my beers?"

"Yeah." Angela nodded and turned away from Vicki's glare to put the beers on Sapphire's tray. She wiped the counter down before facing Vicki again. "What?"

"What? You know what? You're mad because the man said he's falling in love with you and that's why he covered your expenses for the next six months."

"I'm mad because he did that without asking." Angela glanced around the bar to make sure the patrons were okay. For the moment everyone watched one of the dancers and the kitchen hadn't delivered her customer's chicken wings, which gave her a second to focus on Vicki.

"He loves you," Vicki said, as if that explained everything. "He's not just playing around with you. That's why he did it."

"But I don't want to be dependent on him."

"This doesn't make you dependent on him. It makes your life much easier in the next few months while you fight the battle to get full custody of Cory."

Nervous anticipation fluttered in Angela's stomach. "I can't believe I'm really going to be a mom."

She hadn't told Cory, but as she'd explained the situation to Vicki and thought about what could happen to Cory if she didn't, she'd come to an immediate decision. She wouldn't let him be shuffled around by a flighty mother, or sit in a foster home until Darryl was released to do who knew what. He needed stability, someone who wouldn't just dump him, someone he could trust, and she would be that person.

Vicki rubbed Angela's arms. "You'll be a great mom. You already are, and Isaiah's help will make the transition easier."

"But what if I get used to his help and he snatches it away? What if I'm left high and dry and struggling again?"

"Are you going to ask him to always pay your bills?"

"Of course not."

"Then you don't have anything to worry about. He's not going to take over your life unless you let him. And he's not your aunt. He isn't doing you a favor just to turn around and betray you later."

"How do I know that? How do I know if trusting him is the right thing to do? I trusted family and family let me down."

"Your aunt didn't love you," Vicki said simply. "Don't view what she did as an act of a loving person. Isaiah sounds like the kind of man who says what he means without an ulterior motive. Trust your instincts. Do you really think he'll try to take advantage of you, or are you just afraid to finally be in a relationship that will require you to trust him as much as you want to?"

Fear tightened her throat and her chest. She wasn't falling in love with Isaiah, she had already fallen. She could imagine the type of life they could build, a life she wanted, but she was afraid to have that dream shattered.

Vicki must have read her face because her smile was sad. "Sorry, Angela, but sometimes you've got to step out on faith. Plus, how often do you meet a rich guy in a strip club that actually wants to do something besides peel off those wings and take you to bed?" Vicki asked with a grin.

The humor lessened some of the tightness in Angela's chest and she laughed. "That's not why I love him."

"I know, but it's not a bad perk, either."

Z walked over and tapped his knuckles on the bar. "Are we finished with our touching moment?" Despite his words there was a trace of humor in his tone.

"What do you need, Z?" Angela asked.

"Another VIP group came in. Small party. One of the guys on the Gators team. He asked for you to serve the drinks specifically" He looked at Angela.

Angela pointed to her chest. "Why me? It's not Isaiah, is it?"

Z shook his head. "Nah, the new guy traded to them. I don't know why and I don't like the look of him, but I've got no good reason to say you can't. Just bring the drinks and let me know if he gives you any trouble, all right?"

Angela nodded. "I will." Z's bad feelings about customers usually proved to be correct. Angela and Vicki exchanged a look before she grabbed a note pad to write orders on and walked to the VIP.

Bruno stood close to the area. He gave her a reassuring nod before stepping aside to let her by. Some of her unease settled. Bruno didn't care who the customers were—if the guy asking for Angela caused any problems, Bruno would get rid of him.

Angela took a deep breath of the lavender scent in her diffuser charm, pasted on a welcoming smile and walked up to the VIP. The two bodyguards there eyed her white tank top, black skirt and angel's wings with interest, but stepped aside without talking.

"Hello, fellas, I'm Angel and I'm here to take your drink orders." There were four men in the VIP. She recognized the one from the team. A younger player named Mark who dressed in a flashy style meant to show off the millions in his reported contract. The three with him were just as flashy, but didn't look like anyone from the team she recognized and she assumed they were his friends or entourage.

Mark stood, wobbled a bit before he regained his balance. He lifted the shades from bloodshot eyes and licked his lips while he looked at her from head to toe. "Well, well, well, if it isn't Isaiah's own perfect angel."

Angela barely kept her smile on her face. "Can I get you something to drink?"

He stumbled over to her. "Of course. We want four bottles of your best champagne. We're celebrating before heading off to training camp."

Then alcohol probably shouldn't be on his menu. "Okay, I'll be right back." She turned to leave but his hand ran down her back. Angela swung around and glared. "Don't touch me."

He chuckled and his friends followed suit. "Why? Because you're Isaiah's flavor of the month?" He leaned in close. "I know your type. How much for a taste. Let me see what's so good it's got Mr. Perfect all tied up in knots."

"I'll get your champagne and another waitress for you." She turned away again.

He wrapped an arm around her waist and jerked her hard against his body. "Playing hard to get, huh?"

Angela stomach lurched with disgust. She stomped her heel into his foot. He squealed and his grip loosened. She spun and shoved him away with both hands. He was already wobbly on his feet and fell backward into the table with a loud crash. His friends look stunned before they all started laughing and pointing at him. He groaned, lifted his head, then rolled over and threw up on the floor.

The bodyguards and Bruno burst into the room. Bruno immediately moved to stand between Angela and the rest of the guys. "What the hell happened?"

"He grabbed me from behind. I got him off of me," Angela said with no remorse.

"She attacked me," Mark said from where he was bent over on the floor.

Z entered the VIP. "Then let's pull the recording and see exactly what happened."

Mark blanched. "Recording?"

Z nodded. "I record every VIP room for this very reason. I don't like men manhandling my girls. If she attacked you, fine, she'll be dealt with. But if you touched her and she defended herself, we're pressing charges. Of course the video will be released as evidence."

He looked as if he'd throw up again. "To hell with this. Let's get out of here."

"You will get the bill for cleanup," Z said.

After they left, Z took her into his office and gave her a glass of water. Her hands shook as she brought it to her lips. "Are you okay?"

She nodded. "Yeah. He only grabbed me."

"Still, I don't like it when you girls get touched without your consent. Why don't you take the rest of the night off?"

"I don't need to do that. It's Saturday and busy."

"I can handle the bar with Candy. You're shaking, and from the way you and Vicki kept chatting, I can tell something is bothering you. I'd rather you deal with that than stay here and be a half-assed bartender."

The words were gruff, but there was a smile on his hard face and concern in his dark eyes.

"Are you sure?" she asked.

"Get the hell out of here before I change my mind."

Angela smiled and walked over to kiss him on the forehead. "For a sleazy strip-club owner, you're not half-bad."

Z laughed. "Sleazy? I run the best strip club in the area. Don't get it twisted. Now go get some rest. And call your boyfriend before word gets back to him about his teammate and he tries to kick his ass. I need the Gators to make it to the playoffs again, not fight each other and ruin the season."

Angela waved him off and left. Her heart tightened with the idea that Isaiah may not care one way or the other. He'd been angry when she'd kicked him out earlier today. She was still mad he went behind her back and wanted her to quit bartending, but nights like tonight weren't atypical. Every few months she had to fend off some overzealous customer. She was tired of fighting off men. The money was good, and Z was a great boss, but if she was going to give Cory a stable home, she didn't want to keep working late nights. Quitting may be her best choice.

Chapter 27

"She must be the realest woman in the area," Kevin said to Isaiah.

Isaiah paused in making his shot on the pool table. Instead of going to the favorite pool hall the team typically visited after a game, they were playing in Will's game room. Isaiah stood and gave Kevin a confused look. "What?"

Will stood next to Kevin and nodded. "I gotta agree with my man."

"She's mad because I tried to help," Isaiah said in a disbelieving tone of voice. "She kicked me out of her house."

"Let's be real, Isaiah," Kevin said. "How many people do we come across that'll be mad we paid all their bills? Zero to none. You've actually found a woman who doesn't want you to come in and make all her problems disappear with a swipe of your checkbook."

"Are you on her side?" Isaiah asked, frustrated.

"Not really. I get why you did what you did," Will said. "No man is going to sit by and watch his woman struggle if he can help. But the fact that she didn't ask and she's upset means she isn't after you for your money. That's a good thing."

"Did you think she wanted me for my money?"

Will shrugged and ran a hand over his beard. "I mean…that's always a possibility when it comes to the women we meet."

"Yeah," Kevin said. "You've got someone who's real about being with you. That's not something to throw away."

"I didn't throw anything away. She kicked me out."

Kevin held his pool cue in front of him and looked thoughtful. "Any idea why she's mad about you paying her bills for her? I mean, with women there's usually a reason."

Will chuckled. "Usually? I can't agree with that. How about around fifteen percent of the time there's a good reason."

Kevin shook his head and grinned. "Okay, I admit that. So what's her reason?"

Isaiah thought back to what she'd accused him of doing. "She doesn't want to be dependent on me. But that's not what I'm trying to do."

"Why would she think you're doing that?" Kevin put down his cue and walked over. "Come on, man, let's think about this from her side. You be you and I'll be her."

Isaiah laughed. "Are you serious?"

"Hell yeah." Kevin put a hand on his hip and batted his eyes in a bad imitation of a woman. "Isaiah, you can't be ruling my life." He held up a finger and talked in a falsetto voice.

Isaiah and Will both laughed. "I'm not trying to take over your life."

"You're trying to control me," Kevin continued in the same silly tone of voice. "You're trying to run my life just like my…" Kevin's words trailed off.

It hit him like a basketball in the face. "Just like her aunt."

"I can't trust you just like I can't trust her," Kevin continued.

She couldn't trust her aunt. Her brother was in jail and then his girlfriend had moved to New York with no immediate plans to return, leaving her with the responsibility of taking care of Cory. She'd constantly had to handle the consequences of bad decisions made by people she should've been able to trust.

"She thinks I'll move in, pretend to make things better, then leave her high and dry just like everyone else."

Will looked between the two of them. "That actually worked?"

Isaiah shushed him and connected the dots. He told her he was falling in love, honestly loved her a little already, but he'd gone behind her back to do what he wanted anyway. That didn't make it easy to trust him in the future. If she felt like he was stepping in and making things better, but she had no reassurance he wasn't going to leave her hanging like everyone else, then of course she would push him away.

"Damn, how do I show her I'm not going anywhere?" He looked at his friends.

Will shrugged. "I'm not about that monogamous life."

Kevin shook his head. "I'm zero for two with my long-term relationships. But what I will say is be honest with her. Show her you trust her to make her own decisions. Maybe then she'll believe you won't just drop her with all the work."

Isaiah's cell phone rang. He pulled it out. "It's Jacobe." He answered the phone. "You coming to hang out?"

"Nah, I'm calling to see if you've heard about what happened at Sweethearts," Jacobe said in a hesitant voice.

Isaiah's stomach clenched. "What happened?"

"Mark went there with some of his friends. He was drunk and grabbed Angela."

"What?" Isaiah yelled. He looked around for his keys. "I'm going to kill him."

"Calm down, Rambo, apparently she handled it. Left him on the floor throwing up. Lots of damage and one of his *boys* posted the video on Instagram already," Jacobe said with a laugh. "Your girl is pretty badass."

That didn't lessen Isaiah's anger. He was happy to hear she was okay. He was crazy for behaving as if she couldn't handle herself. She wouldn't have been able to work for so long at Sweethearts if she needed a savior. Someone who rebounded after her aunt's betrayal, took in a teenager without argument and fended off idiots like his teammate didn't need a savoir to step in. She only needed a partner. He wanted to be her partner.

"Thanks for telling me. I'm going out there now."

"All right. Just wanted you to hear about it now instead of in the locker room."

"Thanks for looking out," Isaiah said. They got off the phone and he looked at the fellas. "I've got to go check on Angela."

Isaiah hurried out to his vehicle. He went straight to Sweethearts first, but her boss informed him that he'd sent her home for the day.

"Was she okay? Is she hurt?" Isaiah asked.

Z shook his head and chuckled. "Anyone who messes with Angela is more likely to be the one who ends up hurt. She knows how to handle herself. She had your teammate on the floor long before my bouncer could even get in there."

Isaiah's shoulders relaxed hearing that. He smiled and felt a little proud. "Really?"

"You sound surprised. Don't you know you've got a fighter on your hands?"

"I do. It's one of the things I love about her. She doesn't let anything stop her." Including him.

He left Sweethearts and went to Angela's apartment. He thought about what he could say. Obviously he wasn't there to rescue her because she didn't need to be rescued. He had to apologize, hope she was willing to listen and hope he hadn't pushed her away.

His palms were sweaty and his pulse raced when he knocked on her door. Worry that she was okay and concern that she didn't want to see him caused his stomach to clench.

Angela jerked open the door. "Cory?" Her hair was out of place, as if she'd run her hands through it constantly. Her eyes were wide and worried, and she gripped her cell phone in her hand. When she focused on him, her lower lip wobbled and she flung herself into his arms. "Isaiah, Cory is missing."

Chapter 28

Angela didn't care that they were kinda sorta broken up. When she saw Isaiah, she knew he would help her find Cory. Since his fourteenth birthday was the following week, she'd agreed to let him stay home while she worked that night. He'd said he was just going to spend the time playing video games and watching television. He still seemed upset about the phone call with his father and said he didn't want to hang out with Nate. Stupid, stupid, stupid of her to let him stay.

Her mind raced with all the possibilities of what was going on. Had someone knocked on the door and taken him? Had he left to go somewhere and gotten snatched? There was no good reason for him not to be here, which meant there were only bad reasons for him to have left.

Isaiah brought her into the apartment and sat her on the couch. His hands were stable and strong as they pushed the hair away from her face. She drew her first steady breath since coming home and finding Cory missing. Her entire body trembled.

"Now tell me what happened?" he said in a calm voice. He met her eyes and took several deep breaths.

She mirrored his breathing. "I got home about thirty minutes ago. I thought Cory was in his room. I changed, then knocked on his door. He's wasn't there. I called his cell phone, but it's going straight to voice mail. There isn't a note, but when I looked in his closet I noticed his book bag and some clothes are missing." Her voice wobbled. "Where would he go? Do you think someone took him?"

She started to cry. Isaiah took her hand in his. "Shh… don't automatically jump to the worst conclusion," he said in a calm voice. "He's had a rough day. Think back to before you left for work? Did he say or do anything before you left?"

She sucked in a voice and thought back. "He said he was just going to hang out. I think he was texting his girlfriend."

Isaiah's eyes lit up. "His girlfriend."

"What—what do you know?"

"He said earlier this morning that she was the only person who cared for him."

"How could he think that?" Anger mixed with her worry. "Of course I care about him. I love him. I'm going to try and adopt him!"

"You told him that?"

Her shoulders slumped. Fresh tears popped up. "Not yet."

Isaiah wiped her tears away. "He's confused and worried right now. He thinks Denise isn't obligated to care for him. I'd bet money that's where he went."

"Where does she live?" Angela jumped up from the chair. "Let's go get him right now. If he's not dead I'm going to kill him for scaring me."

"I don't know where she lives, but we can call Keri. She'll have the registration for all the kids and might be able to give us a phone number if not an address once we explain what's going on."

Angela nodded. "Call her."

Isaiah got on the phone and Angela bit her lip to keep from asking him to repeat everything Keri said. It took a bit of convincing, but Keri agreed to at least go to the office and pull a number for Denise's parents.

"We'll meet her at the center," Angela said after he hung up.

"What if he comes back?" Isaiah said. "Someone should be here."

Angela ran her fingers through her hair again. "Crap! This is why I'm going to make a terrible mother. I shouldn't have left him home."

"He's almost fourteen. You didn't do anything wrong to trust him."

"I shouldn't be working at night."

"You provide for him by doing that. You're not the only guardian that has to work at night. You're doing everything you can to take care of Cory. Don't beat yourself up."

The door opened and Cory walked in. Angela ran over to him. "Cory, thank God!" She grasped his shoulders and looked him over from head to toe. No bruises, thankfully, but he had his book bag on his shoulder. She let him go and smacked his arm. "Where in the world have you been? I've been worried sick."

"I'm sorry," Cory said. "I thought… I wasn't sure if I should stay?"

"So you were going to run away? Are you crazy? Why would you do that?"

Cory looked at the floor. "My dad's in jail. My mom doesn't want me. I'm just a burden on everyone. I can take care of myself."

"So can I, but that doesn't mean I can't accept a little help sometimes from the people who love me. I love you, Cory." His head shot up and surprise filled his eyes.

"Don't look shocked. It's true. I want legal guardianship of you."

"You do?" he sounded hopeful.

"Yes. I'm not going to leave you high and dry. We've made out pretty well this summer—no need to mess that up."

The hope in his eyes faded. "What if my mom says no?"

"We'll deal with that when we get in touch with her." Angela doubted Heather would say no. Not after she dumped Cory off without a look back. "Even if she does, I'm not going to lose touch with you. I promised to take care of you and I mean it." Tears ran down her face. She was so thankful he was safe.

Cory's eyes widened at her tears. He shuffled his feet and touched her arm. "I'm sorry I scared you, Auntie. I don't want to be your burden."

Angela swiped the tears from her face. "You're not a burden. I want you here. I love you."

Cory's eyes glittered. He lowered them and sniffed loudly through his nose. Angela pulled him into a hug. He hugged her back. "If you ever run away again I'm hunting you down so I can skin you."

He chuckled and nodded. "I won't run again." He stepped back and met her eye.

Isaiah came up behind her and placed his hand on her shoulder. "Good. Running away from your problem doesn't solve it."

"Unless you're being chased by a bear," Cory said.

Angela shook her head but smiled. "This is not the time for jokes." Her smile went away. "We're serious. Understand?"

Cory nodded. "I understand."

"Go put your stuff up and then we'll talk some more," Isaiah said.

Cory squeezed Angela's hand, then went to his room. Angela let out a deep breath. "If he hadn't come back..."

"But he did. And we'll make sure he understands we mean it when we say we won't put up with him running off just because he's upset."

"We?" Her voice croaked. She cleared her throat. Damn tears.

Isaiah took her hands in his. "Yes, we. If you'll forgive me."

"What am I forgiving you for?" She was the one who'd kicked him out.

"I shouldn't have paid your bills without talking to you first. I'll admit I'm ready to settle down. I want to have what my parents have. I want a family. Maybe I saw you and Cory and when I fell in love, I thought my family was ready. I should have consulted you on that first. I don't want to take over your life. I want to be your partner in it. I want to talk about what's going on and we work together for a solution. Not be the one making all the decisions."

The happiness those words inspired in her was almost more than she could contain. "What about my job at Sweethearts?"

He took a deep breath. "It's obvious you can take care of yourself. I heard about what Mark did."

She frowned, then waved her hand. "That. I'd forgotten about it as soon as I got here and realized Cory was missing."

"Still, I don't like the idea of someone threatening you. I can't lie, but that is your source of income. If you decide to stay there, I know you can handle yourself," he said without a trace of insincerity.

"I've already decided that once I'm finished with school I'm done. I don't want to work the late hours anymore or deal with guys like Jerry or Mark. Until then, I need the income. You paid for my larger expenses, but there are others. Can you deal with that for just a few more months?"

He tugged on her hands until only inches separated them. "I deal with a lot more if it means you've forgiven me?"

"Only if you forgive me. I overreacted earlier today. I was upset about my family, it brought up old memories and I took that out on you."

"I don't want you to do what I say or else. I love you and I want us to be equals in everything we do, especially when it comes to our relationship. Actions speak louder than words. I'm ready to work hard and go into overtime to show how much I love you."

He kissed her. Angela wrapped her arms around his neck and pressed close to him. She let go of the fear and mistrust in her heart. She'd trust this.

"Ewww!" Cory's voice interrupted. "Am I going to always have to break up you guys kissing?"

Angela and Isaiah broke apart, but he still held her against his side. "Get used to that, kiddo. We're going to be together a while."

Cory's eyes widened. He looked at Isaiah, then at Angela. "For real?"

"Is that okay with you?" Isaiah asked.

Cory considered that, then grinned. "As long as you keep the kissing to behind closed doors."

Isaiah laughed and turned Angela in his arms. "Sorry, Cory, I can't promise you that." He kissed her again, and this time, Cory just smiled.

Epilogue

"If you get eaten by a shark in the middle of the season, Coach Gray is going to kill me," Angela said with a nervous smile.

Isaiah and Cory both laughed. The early-spring morning was temperate and the breeze carried the scent of the ocean to where they stood on the dock waiting as the film crew prepared the boat to film the sharks migrating south along the coastline. Isaiah and Cory were both dressed in swim trunks and long-sleeved T-shirts.

Isaiah pulled Angela into a hug and kissed her forehead. "Don't worry, Angel. I'm just going to watch them film and maybe throw out a little chum."

Cory bounced on his toes. "You've gotta go down in the cage."

Angela shook her head. "No cages. Just watch and enjoy." She pointed at Cory. "Especially you. Don't even lean on the edge of the boat."

Isaiah chuckled. "It's not that big a deal. We're just capturing the migration. Cory, why don't you take our book bag on board while I reassure your aunt."

Cory picked up the book bag and smirked. "While you kiss her again. Thanks for the heads-up this time." He hesitated, then walked forward and kissed Angela's cheek. "Don't worry, I won't let him get a hand bitten off." Cory grinned, then turned and went to the ship.

Tears pricked Angela's eyes and she touched the spot on her cheek where he'd kissed her. "I guess he's still happy with me."

Isaiah ran a comforting hand up and down her back. "I think so. I'm glad Heather agreed to temporary guardianship."

Angela nodded and watched Cory talk to some of the crew. "I am, too, but I'm still disappointed in her. Guardianship until Darryl is out of jail is guardianship until Cory's graduating high school. I knew she was selfish, but still."

"Shh." Isaiah turned her to face him and kissed her forehead. "It's all for the best. Everything is turning out well, Ms. Assistant Director," he added with a grin.

Angela was happy to take her mind off her disappointment and switch to the good news she'd gotten the other day. She'd accepted the job of assistant director at the North Region Activity Center and started in two weeks. She was nervous and excited. Getting fired from working as an advocate still annoyed her, but she would get to work with kids in the community and that was what mattered.

"I can't believe it, but I'm ready for the challenge. School's done, I've got a new job and Cory is settled and happy. Everything is great."

"There's one other thing I think would make things even better."

She placed her hands on his chest. His heart beat fast beneath her palms. Frowning, she noticed nervousness in his eyes. "What's wrong?"

Isaiah licked his lips. His hands squeezed her hips. "I love you, Angela. I want to marry you." Her jaw dropped and he continued in a rush. "I know we had a whirlwind relationship and you're finally getting back on your feet, but that doesn't change how I feel about you. I want us to be permanent partners in life and in love."

"When?" Her face broke out into a huge smile. Her own heart matched the pace of his.

"After the season. When we've got time to plan and decide how we want to move forward with starting our lives together—maybe growing our family."

"I didn't know if I ever wanted to get married, much less have kids. I was afraid I wouldn't be able to trust anyone enough to fully combine my life with theirs. But, Isaiah, you've shown me that you don't want to run my life."

"I'm sorry about the rent and school."

She shook her head. "That's over and done with. Honestly, it helped out a lot and I can never repay you for helping me out the way you did. Since then you've shown me that you respect my decisions. We talk things out, you're always there for Cory and you haven't pushed even when I knew you wanted to. I want to marry you, too, Isaiah. I want to build a family with you."

The smile on his face turned her world into a kaleidoscope of colors. "Is that a yes?"

Angela grinned and nodded. "Yes."

"Yes!" Isaiah picked her up and swung her around.

Angela yelped, then wrapped her arms around his neck. She laughed and held him tight, feeling safe and protected in the security of his arms.

"She said yes?" It was Cory's voice.

Isaiah put down Angela. "She did."

She looked at her nephew's eager grin and Isaiah's matching one. "You knew he was going to ask?"

"Of course. I'm the man of the house," Cory said, tugging proudly on the front of his shirt.

"Okay, man." Angela rolled her eyes, then pulled Cory into a hug.

Isaiah wrapped his arms around both of them for a group hug. Angela's body sang with love and contentment. She didn't have to do things alone anymore. She had a family she could count on, and she believed with her whole heart in this chance at love she'd been given.

* * * * *

KIMANI™
ROMANCE

COMING NEXT MONTH
Available January 16, 2018

#557 HER UNEXPECTED VALENTINE
Bare Sophistication • by Sherelle Green

Nicole LeBlanc lands a coveted gig as lead makeup artist and hairstylist on a series of Valentine's Day commercials. Once she meets the creative director, she's certain he could fulfill her romantic fantasies. Nicole tempts Kendrick Burrstone to take another chance at love…until a media frenzy jeopardizes it all.

#558 BE MY FOREVER BRIDE
The Kingsleys of Texas • by Martha Kennerson

It was like a fairy tale: eloping with Houston oil tycoon Brice Kingsley. Then a devastating diagnosis and a threat from her past forced Brooke Smith Kingsley to leave. Now she can make things right, but only if she can keep her secret—and her distance—from her irresistible husband.

#559 ON-AIR PASSION
The Clarks of Atlanta • by Lindsay Evans

Ahmed Clark left sports to become a radio show host—one who's cynical about romance. But when Elle Marshall goes on air to promote her business, they clash and sizzle over the airwaves. Putting his heart in play is his riskiest move, but it's the only way to win hers…

#560 A TASTE OF DESIRE
Deliciously Dechamps • by Chloe Blake

International real estate agent Nicole Parks isn't expecting romance in Brazil, but she's falling for French vintner Destin Dechamps. Yet he's out to sabotage the deal that will guarantee her a promotion and the adoption she's been longing for. With their dreams in the balance, is there room for love?

Get 2 Free Books,
Plus 2 Free Gifts—
just for trying the
Reader Service!

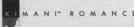

KIMANI™ ROMANCE

YES! Please send me 2 FREE Harlequin® Kimani™ Romance novels and my 2 FREE gifts (gifts are worth about $10 retail). After receiving them, if I don't wish to receive any more books, I can return the shipping statement marked "cancel." If I don't cancel, I will receive 4 brand-new novels every month and be billed just $5.69 per book in the U.S. or $6.24 per book in Canada. That's a savings of at least 12% off the cover price. It's quite a bargain! Shipping and handling is just 50¢ per book in the U.S. and 75¢ per book in Canada*. I understand that accepting the 2 free books and gifts places me under no obligation to buy anything. I can always return a shipment and cancel at any time. The free books and gifts are mine to keep no matter what I decide.

168/368 XDN GMWW

Name   (PLEASE PRINT)

Address   Apt. #

City   State/Prov.   Zip/Postal Code

Signature (if under 18, a parent or guardian must sign)

Mail to the **Reader Service:**
IN U.S.A.: P.O. Box 1341, Buffalo, NY 14240-8531
IN CANADA: P.O. Box 603, Fort Erie, Ontario L2A 5X3

Want to try two free books from another line?
Call 1-800-873-8635 or visit www.ReaderService.com.

*Terms and prices subject to change without notice. Prices do not include applicable taxes. Sales tax applicable in NY. Canadian residents will be charged applicable taxes. Offer not valid in Quebec. This offer is limited to one order per household. Books received may not be as shown. Not valid for current subscribers to Harlequin® Kimani™ Romance books. All orders subject to approval. Credit or debit balances in a customer's account(s) may be offset by any other outstanding balance owed by or to the customer. Please allow 4 to 6 weeks for delivery. Offer available while quantities last.

Your Privacy—The Reader Service is committed to protecting your privacy. Our Privacy Policy is available online at www.ReaderService.com or upon request from the Reader Service.

We make a portion of our mailing list available to reputable third parties that offer products we believe may interest you. If you prefer that we not exchange your name with third parties, or if you wish to clarify or modify your communication preferences, please visit us at www.ReaderService.com/consumerchoice or write to us at Reader Service Preference Service, P.O. Box 9062, Buffalo, NY 14240-9062. Include your complete name and address.

KROM17R3

SPECIAL EXCERPT FROM

It was like something out of a fairy tale: being swept off her feet, then eloping with her one true love, Houston oil tycoon Brice Kingsley. Then a devastating diagnosis and a threat from her past forced Brooke Smith Kingsley to leave the man she loved. Now she has a chance to make things right, but only if she can keep her secret—and her distance—from her irresistible husband.

Read on for a sneak peek at
BE MY FOREVER BRIDE, the next exciting
installment in author Martha Kennerson's
***THE KINGSLEYS OF TEXAS** series!*

Brooke opened the door and walked into the office to find Brice seated behind his desk, signing several documents. "Did you forget something, Amy?"

The sound of his voice sent waves of desire throughout her body, just like they had from the first moment they met. She'd missed it… She'd missed him. "It's not Amy, Brice," Brooke replied, closing the door behind her, knowing this conversation wasn't for the public.

Brice dropped his pen, raised his head and sat back in his seat. "Brooke," he said, his face expressionless.

"Do you have a moment for a quick chat?" She tried to project confidence when in reality she was a nervous wreck inside. Her heart was beating so fast she just knew the whole building could hear it.

Brice tilted his head slightly to the right and his forehead crinkled. "You tell me after six months of what I thought was a wonderful marriage that you want out. I convince you to give us time to work things out—at least I thought I had—and go out for your favorite seafood only to come back to find that you've left me with a note." He leaned forward slightly. "You disappear for three months, only communicating through your lawyer, and now you want to chat." His tone was hard but even.

"I…I—"

"Sure, please have a seat." His words were laced with disdain and sarcasm.

Brooke moved forward on unsteady legs, reaching for the support of a chair. She swallowed hard. "You make it sound so—"

"So what? Honest? Is that not what happened?"

"I didn't want to fight. Not then and certainly not now," she explained, trying to hold his angry glare.

"What *do* you want, Brooke?" Brice asked, sitting back in his chair.

"It's simple. I'd like to get through these next several weeks as painlessly as possible. We're both professionals with a job to do."

Brice sat up in his chair. "That we are." He reached into his desk drawer and pulled out a manila envelope. "We can start by you signing the settlement papers so the lawyers can move forward with the divorce."

Don't miss BE MY FOREVER BRIDE
by Martha Kennerson, available February 2018
wherever Harlequin® Kimani Romance™
books and ebooks are sold!

Copyright © 2018 Martha Kennerson

KPEXP0118

Want to give in to temptation with
steamy tales of irresistible desire?

Check out **Harlequin® Presents®**,
Harlequin® Desire and
Harlequin® Kimani™ Romance books!

New books available every month!

CONNECT WITH US AT:

Harlequin.com/Community

 Facebook.com/HarlequinBooks

 Twitter.com/HarlequinBooks

 Instagram.com/HarlequinBooks

 Pinterest.com/HarlequinBooks

ReaderService.com

**ROMANCE WHEN
YOU NEED IT**

PGENRE2017

LOVE
Harlequin
romance?

Join our Harlequin community to share your thoughts and connect with other romance readers!

Be the first to find out about promotions, news, and exclusive content!

Sign up for the Harlequin e-newsletter and download a free book from any series at

www.TryHarlequin.com

CONNECT WITH US AT:

Harlequin.com/Community

 Facebook.com/HarlequinBooks

 Twitter.com/HarlequinBooks

 Instagram.com/HarlequinBooks

 Pinterest.com/HarlequinBooks

ReaderService.com

**ROMANCE WHEN
YOU NEED IT**

HSOCIAL2017

Reward the book lover in you!

Earn points from all your Harlequin book purchases from wherever you shop.

Turn your points into *FREE BOOKS* of your choice
OR
EXCLUSIVE GIFTS from your favorite authors or series.

Join for FREE today at
www.HarlequinMyRewards.com.

Harlequin My Rewards is a free program (no fees) without any commitments or obligations.

MYR17